Antique and Deadly

ANTIQUE AND DEADLY

Lucine Hansz Flynn

Walker and Company
New York

First published in the United States of America in 1988 by the Walker Publishing Company, Inc.

Published simultaneously in Canada by Thomas Allen & Son Canada, Limited, Markham, Ontario.

Library of Congress Cataloging-in-Publication Data
Flynn, Lucine Hansz.
    Antique and deadly.

    I. Title.
PS3556.L88A85   1988   813'.54   87-37179
ISBN 0-8027-5702-2

Printed in the United States of America

10 9 8 7 6 5 4 3 2 1

1

ONE SOFT TUESDAY morning in April, I was polishing the last of three dozen assorted wineglasses intended to add sparkle to my antique shop window, when Cora Whitney bustled in. She's a dumpy little woman who habitually opens her eyes wide when she talks, denoting interest, agreement, surprise, disbelief—anything—and she goes through life under a continuous full head of steam.

"Susan! I can't stay—don't have a shop-sitter. Just ran across to tell you! Old Joe Foster's dead!" Cora is at least fifty-five. No amount of pressure can make her admit to more than forty-two.

The fragile stem of the wineglass snapped in my fingers.

"Oh, my dear!" The faded brown eyes opened wide. Cora fluttered a hand at the broken glass. "I'm so sorry. You must let me buy it from you."

Well, yes. Now that she mentioned it, I had every intention of selling to Cora Whitney one broken wineglass. Silently I returned thanks that it wasn't one of the set I had laboriously assembled and which was without flaw.

"A quarter?"

"Don't be silly. Three bucks."

Cora Whitney vented a small ladylike scream. "Three dollars! Thirty cents."

Twenty minutes of hard bargaining brought us to meet at a dollar-sixty, which was about what Cora expected to pay and about what I anticipated getting for it.

I found a little box and wrapped the two segments, discounting the while Cora's breathless murmurs of impending bankruptcy. I knew full well that Cora Whitney would cement the pieces together and sell that glass for about four dollars as one whose stem had been snapped by George Washington after a sentimental toast. She wouldn't say so, but her vaporings would convey that message, and she'd realize a markup of two hundred fifty percent.

Handing over the parcel completed the transaction. Cora switched off her prophesies of personal doom and returned to her purpose for calling.

"I'm so sorry," she said again, "I should have remembered how much Old Joe meant to you. But Susan, dear, try to look on his passing as a blessing. He was so very sick, you know."

Cora patted my arm with all the solicitude normally reserved for grieving widows, blinked rapidly as through tears, and bustled out, turning, when she gained the sidewalk, toward the Thornton's "Stuff and Things."

Pete Thornton calls her the town crier of Belmont Street. No one ever asks how Cora finds out. She simply knows.

Joe Foster had been very sick indeed since his first stroke four months earlier. Dying while still short of sixty was sad, but four months with one side paralyzed and speech so impaired as to be well-nigh unintelligible were ample. He knew from the beginning that there was no getting well for Joe Foster.

So it wasn't grief that snapped the wineglass, although grief would come later. It wasn't even surprise. We had all known about the second stroke day before yesterday. Rather, it was—well, call it an involuntary salute to the end of an era. There was no denying that Belmont Street would be different, and less, without Joe Foster.

Belmont Street, three blocks long, dead-ends at both ends and is pierced twice along its length by cross streets so narrow that they can accommodate one car's passage, if the driver is careful, or one pedestrian's progress, if he's reasonably sober, but not, simultaneously, a drunken pedestrian and heedless driver. Those two narrow streets

2

look like alleys, and that's how they're used.

Belmont Street, however, is not an alley and has never been one. Neither is it an Indian warpath that worked up to urban status. Belmont from its inception was a city street with some claim to elegance. Two- and three-story brick town houses, some with bowed windows and some that are flat fronted, line both sides of the street, going up flush with the sidewalks, which are also brick. Belmont Street's bricks glow pink or rosy beige in the sun, warm and mellow, except for a few places where the houses were painted white or cream or gray. It's a nice street, conveying some of its original air of elegance even in its present reduced station.

Joe Foster was the last to maintain his entire house as his own dwelling. The Foster house had been painted pale gray with spanking white trim and bright green door. From its imposing corner location diagonally across the intersection from Beckett's, the Foster house was a constant reminder of Belmont's former eminence as an in-town address. Joe had lived there all his life. Belmont Street took for granted that family ties were what kept him in the old house. I'm sure that was a factor stiffening his resistance when Margaret wanted to move farther out, but I also thought that Joe insisted on staying—one of the few times he did insist on anything to Margaret—simply because the house was paid for. He made his money in real estate. In the early years he bought heavily discounted second mortgages and collected on them to the last penny. Later, he dealt mostly in commercial properties. Although never so far-seeing as to buy raw land by the acre and sell it by the square foot, Joe Foster nonetheless did very well. Along the way he acquired a lively awareness of the delights of a paid-up mortgage.

Now Joe Foster's house would take the conversion route of the rest of the street. Since neither Ray nor Betty had any interest in living there, the Foster house would fare rather worse than some. Worse, say, than that of the Misses Sanders at the end of the street. They have been reduced to sharing

3

their first floor while living on the revenues produced by motley tenants above them, but their every spare penny goes to "keep up" the premises. Or worse, for that matter, than Beckett's. I live over the shop, but, by God, I also "keep up." Who would keep up Joe Foster's place, with Joe no longer there? Soon it would turn into a shabby parody of itself. The spacious second floor could be made to yield two apartments, but the street floor would more likely go for another shop.

Every city of sufficient size has its Belmont Street, differing in name and details of appearance but essentially much alike. They're often found in old neighborhoods on the way down. They may have been fashionable once, and may be again. If they're still standing when the pendulum starts its next swing, their next incarnation will be expensive. Meanwhile, they exist as Belmont Street, when to say the name is to identify the activity. Because they are no longer chic, rents are not prohibitively high and zoning variances on use not too hard to obtain. Because they aren't out-and-out slums the rats aren't yet so numerous as to eat up the merchandise before it can be sold.

To the unknowing the merchandise is junk. Much of it started as somebody's discard, and it's axiomatic that what A throws away B can sell to C. To the collector hooked on a hobby or inflamed by hope of gain, Belmont Street's wares, down to the last rusty cotter pin, are antiques. Some of the stuff may be antique. Much of it is not. Either way, profits are there, but not as a rule to the ardent soul fondling his three hundred whiskey bottles because they're worth up to thirty clams apiece. He is C in the equation. Money flows from, not to, the C's.

It's the B's who make money. Like me: Susan Beckett; twenty-seven; five-six; reasonably thin at a hundred and thirty; brown hair and gray eyes and skin that I've been told is very fine. I sound like a catalog entry of myself.

Well, I spend a lot of time with catalogs.

I left out the most important authenticating item, though: daughter of Dr. Henry (Hank to his friends) Beckett. Hank Beckett, appraiser of antiques, especially American-made furniture of the Queen Anne, Chippendale, and Federal periods, was one of a dozen men in America whose word constituted a court of last resort on the question of whether some object was as old as it was claimed to be and how much, therefore, it was worth. The question comes up rather often among prudent buyers with a price range from several hundred to several thousands of dollars.

Hank Beckett was quick to say that he could be fooled. It didn't happen very often. Since he was usually called in by the buyer in an impending transaction, a few sellers turned sullen when that tidy sum disappeared over the horizon. They didn't complain, however, for they never knew when they might want to consult Hank in their turn.

Only once did anyone try to bribe Hank Beckett, murmuring, under cover of keys jingled in a pocket, of fifteen hundred dollars looking for a new home.

Dr. Henry Beckett straightened to his full six-feet-three and turned his scholarly gray eyes on the dealer in a long thoughtful look, while the other jingled his keys in furious embarrassment and slowly turned bright pink.

"Sorry," mumbled the dealer when he could stand Hank's benign gaze no longer. "Let's just forget it, shall we?"

"Thank you," said soft-spoken Dr. Beckett. "Much the better course." Then he went back to examining the medallion-back sofa offered as bearing the original finish *and upholstery*, a combination fairly rare and also fairly ugly. The sofa needed a new cover. The odd part was that the sofa was genuine.

The dealer broke into a gentle perspiration of relief when Hank voiced his opinion, at the same time casting him a glance of gratitude mixed with bridled rage.

On the way home Hank answered my nine-year-old un-

5

certainty over what that sweaty little man was so mad about. Mother had died the year before, and taking me along was Hank's solution to the baby-sitter problem. That, and treating me as a chosen comrade, a comradeship that was strengthened, not diminished, when I took my little-girl tragedies and tears to Hank for repair. He'd pick me up and dust me off, so to speak, and then ask, matter-of-fact and man-to-man, "Okay, now?"

So I knew he'd give me a straight answer about the little man who acted so mad all of a sudden.

"Well, you see, he had just given away his reputation as an honest man, and he felt uncomfortable without it." After an interval while he shifted gears with a dreadful grinding of abused metal, he continued, "Integrity's what it's all about, Susan. What's the largest sum of money you can think of, kitten?"

"Oh! A million—no, a *zillion* million dollars!"

"A zillion million. That's quite a lot. Now remember this, Susan. You can't buy your own integrity, not even for all that, but you can sell it for a penny, or you can give it away, as that man at the shop did." Another interval while he swung a triumphant left turn across three lanes of traffic and then Hank went on, more to himself than to me. "I daresay that chap was proud of his reputation for honesty and fair dealing. He was worried about the wrong thing. If he had concentrated on just being honest, and been content with that, his reputation would have been secure. As it is, instead of having both his honesty and his reputation, he has neither."

"Why, Daddy? Because you found him out? Because you know?"

"Eh?" Hank remembered my presence. "Oh, no, Susan, much worse than that. Because *he* knows."

All of which made Hank Beckett's tragic mistake eight years later all the harder to understand.

I no longer tagged after him every waking hour of every

summer and weekend, but was instead in Maine with a school friend at the time, so I didn't see any of what happened. I only heard about it in disjointed snippets.

The sorry sequence started when the Fosters, Joe and Margaret, ran across a Chippendale highboy that looked very fine to their inexpert eyes. The price was eight thousand dollars. They turned, naturally, to their old friend and neighbor, Hank Beckett. Hank looked it over and said they had found a bargain. The Fosters handed over their check on the spot. Everybody was happy. Hank Beckett had done a favor for old friends. The Fosters owned the highboy they coveted, its value now enhanced by Hank's appraisal.

Then Hank hung a "Closed for Vacation" sign on the door of the shop and went off to the West Coast for six weeks of museum hopping and gossip with old cronies. Joe Foster spent some time in New York on business. Margaret's picture graced the society pages. To the extent permitted by frail health—Margaret Foster was in and out of hospitals for thirty years—she enjoyed a position as patroness of the arts while knowing virtually nothing about any one of them.

However, when she assembled a dinner party to show off the Foster's new treasure, she could count on a few who knew antiques—who as one man looked at that damned highboy and then tactfully averted their eyes and talked about something else. Oh, it was Chippendale, all right. It wasn't a fake. Chippendale mostly isn't. A lot of it looks like Grand Rapids '29, but if it's old, then it's pretty apt to be a specimen of the real McCoy. The Foster highboy wasn't a reproduction, either. It was a Chippendale antique. It just wasn't as fine as Joe and Margaret Foster thought and not nearly as fine as Hank Beckett's appraisal said it was. Worth maybe a fourth of what they had paid for it.

It was a mistake anyone could make—anyone but Hank Beckett. The Fosters had turned to him for his superior judgment, and Hank, incredibly, had blown his trust. Another version spread like the wind, that he knew what he had done and was paid to do it. Hank Beckett did not suffer fools gladly, so there were those around town who enjoyed a chance to get their own back at his expense. I was several years older than seventeen before I understood that.

Margaret and Joe couldn't have been nicer about the whole sorry episode. Joe Foster gave it about that anybody was entitled to a few mistakes, including his good friend Hank Beckett, and removed the offending piece from view. As long as Joe Foster lived I never saw that highboy, although I was morally certain that he still had it. The Foster house was jam-packed with the fruits of thirty-five years of steady buying. The Chippendale highboy was there, somewhere.

By easy and rapid degrees the Fosters' magnanimous defense of Hank's wrong call metamorphosed into the flawed judgment of a sick man, for my father very shortly was sick, suffering the first heart attack only four days after he got home from California. With the wisdom of hindsight, everybody talked about how tired he had been looking for months. I soon learned to recognize the meaning of blueness about lips and nails and of the harsh sound of labored breathing. I've always believed that Hank Beckett kept himself alive those last four months by willpower alone. Pain never left his eyes, and a certain remoteness came into his manner, from his awareness, I supposed, of death waiting at his elbow.

The antiques world accepted Hank's bad heart with something near gratitude. I didn't understand that either at the time. Seventeen was too young to understand the frame of mind that says to itself at the edge of awareness, "It may be true, probably is, but I'm half-ashamed for saying it."

Betty was the exception to shame. Adopted daughter of Joe Foster's brother, she was living with her aunt and uncle while she went to college. In retrospect, I suspected that she had been shipped away from an unpromising early romance. Her harried parents needn't have worried. Her eyes rested

8

on Ray Foster before she got her bags unpacked. Betty was two years older than I, at an age when two years made a difference. Even so, she should have saved her war paint. Ray Foster was mine.

She waylaid me in the Foster hall one day when I stopped in with a report on Hank's progress, and after conventional inquiry about Hank, said, "Well, you and your father are lucky at that," and when I gaped at her, added with a sparkle of pure malice, "The kickback from the dealer who sold Uncle Joe the highboy must be coming in pretty handy. What was it, fifty percent?"

"You're lying! Hank never did!"

I didn't see the other Fosters that day, but hared straight across town to another of Hank's friends, charged through the galleries of the fine arts wing to the office in the depths marked "Curator, Fine Arts," and barged in.

"Mr. Limkin, everybody's saying Hank called the Foster highboy wrong on purpose for part of the take."

After a single penetrating glance, Mr. Limkin rallied as a friend. "Who says? Put that right out of your mind, Susan. Your father's a very sick man—*that's* what everybody's saying. How is Hank today?"

Comforting, so that I didn't notice that Mr. Limkin had not quite answered the question, and when, a week or so later, Joe Foster joined his avowals to Mr. Limkin's, I was again comforted. At seventeen I had to believe.

I had been fifteen when we moved our living quarters to the second floor, turned the ground floor into a shop, and hung out our sign. I had finished high school early, having done two years in one a couple of times, and Hank was preoccupied over what to do with me. I was too young to go away to college. Besides, there wasn't enough money. Hank ordered the sign painted and hung without consulting me: Beckett's, of Belmont.

"The apostrophe should come after the *s*," I protested,

when he called me to see our new badge of identity. "There are two of us Becketts."

"For a time, Susan," he said in a matter-of-fact tone. "For a time. It's your shop, really. I'm not young, kitten—" the childhood endearment unaccountably made me blink back tears—"and I don't have much insurance to leave you. Only knowledge."

"You're fine, Hank, don't talk like that."

"I'm tired, Susan. Tired. And—you never know."

Hank was adamant. All that I had soaked up through my pores from those early years of tagging after him was now reinforced and augmented by systematic teaching, as Hank sought to pass on to his daughter everything he knew about American antique furniture. I learned by explicit choice to place quality ahead of age or rarity, to value unity of design above mere complexity without despising the complex, and to hold them both of no account in the face of poor craftsmanship.

"A chair that was poorly designed and poorly made a hundred years ago, Susan, isn't improved just because it's a hundred years old. It's still a poor chair. It isn't enough to sense the difference. You must know, and be able to state why."

Or, "Mediocre carving doesn't become excellent merely because there's a lot of it. But fine carving won't hide bad proportion."

Or, "Pay attention to feet, Susan. If you can distinguish the different feet, you're halfway there to knowing the piece."

"How many kinds of feet are there, Hank?"

"Four hundred," said Hank Beckett austerely.

Much of Hank's encyclopedic knowledge depended on the existence of museum pieces signed by master craftsmen of bygone generations and available for study and comparison. And so, over my heated protests at leaving him, Hank sent me for weeks at a time to Boston and New York,

10

to the Smithsonian in Washington, to Winterthur in Delaware, and to Colonial Williamsburg in Virginia, where Hank's name passed me behind the scenes for intensive tutoring by artisans long dead.

"Use your eyes, Susan," he would admonish before I left home, "but close them, too, and get the feel of age, and the smell of it."

Gradually, I did learn to run my hands over a piece, lightly, lightly caressing the wood, and feel the minute variations in surface wrought by patient years of hand waxing and polishing, incapable of duplication by machines. I caught the odor of old wood, and learned to know at a glance whether I looked at the lovely mellow depth of patina or some latter-day attempt to imitate it.

Hank spent some time on faking. "It's been going on since Egypt was the center of civilization." He sounded very tired. "You'll have to know the ways of the faker."

Hank's mind ran a lot on fakes. "The hardest to detect, Susan, are the ones made long enough ago to have acquired their own patina. I don't mean stuff that started life as honest reproductions. Saw marks will give them away, like as not, or dovetails, and why not? Nobody was trying to hide anything. No, it's the ones that were intended to deceive. Magnificent work in some of them," he observed dispassionately, "always seemed a pity to see it used that way."

A bit diffidently, I asked, "What does give them away, Hank? How can you be sure?"

"Sometimes you can't be certain. You have to let the piece itself tell you, listen to what it says. We're all children of our own time, Susan, with no getting away from that. Assuming the skill is present, it's easy enough for one so minded to decide to do an early Queen Anne slant-top desk exactly as they were done when they were new on the scene. Same choices of wood, same methods in construction, same finish, same everything. No one will ever know. Ah, but everything is not the same, Susan. It's a different age, our man sees the world differently, and he'll build that difference into the desk in spite of himself. For instance, he may build his desk to stand a bit higher from the floor than it should. People on the average have grown a little taller, you see. I can't tell you what to look for, Susan, every case is different. You must listen to the piece and heed what it tells you. It's very easy to go wrong."

Fifteen was too young to live away from home, but not too young to fall in love when Ray came to take me out for dinner and dancing, with me all zinged up in a long dress—pink lace over crepe with very short puffed sleeves and a neckline not quite off the shoulders. I thought it was cut daringly low.

I knew how to dance. Hank had focused on me when I was twelve and said, abstractedly, "Social graces. You should be learning social graces," and packed me off to dancing school twice a week. So I wasn't worried about tripping over my skirt or stepping on my partner's feet. And I had known Ray all my life. But the occasion was a first.

"Do I look all right, Hank?"

"You look fine, kitten. You're growing up. There're stars in your eyes, Susan, you're beautiful."

Then the doorbell sounded and I went down. There was Ray correctly turned out in a tux, and I knew it wasn't a first time for him. Suddenly, he wasn't Ray Foster, old buddy, he was—why, he was an Older Man, come to take *me* out. Tall and slim, like Hank, and handsome, his good looks backlighted by the streetlight, he was a young Lancelot. Come to take *me* out! Only Lancelot's horse was invisible to my enchanted eyes.

"Take good care of her, and try to bring her home by midnight."

"Yes, sir, I'll be very careful," said Ray in the deepened voice of nineteen.

The two men shook hands, as though sealing a pact.

We ate lobster Newburg and mushrooms with walnuts and

peach Melba. Ray had a whiskey sour and I had Rhine wine so light it was grape juice with a little fizz, but oh! I could feel the fizz. We danced every dance when we weren't eating.

"You're a very good dancer," Ray said approvingly from his superior inches. "Our steps just fit. We'll have to do this often."

I danced on air the rest of the evening, and the ones that followed, too.

"We were made to dance through life together, Susan."

I fell ever deeper in love.

Hank saw how it was with me—I was pretty transparent. Part of the reason for those lengthy museum study tours was to supply cooling off periods so I could catch my breath. Only I never did. Ray was mine and I was his. I went, and studied faithfully to please Hank, and wrote long letters in the evening to Hank and to Ray.

I remembered what Hank said about faking when the Foster highboy went sour. Was that what had happened? A fake, so perfectly done so long ago that Hank Beckett was fooled into a mistake. It must have been that. Hank made a mistake. Certainly. Mostly, I tried hard not to think about it.

I was three months shy of eighteen, and Hank just home from the hospital, when he urged me to apply for membership in the professional association of appraisers.

"You'll pass the test blindfolded, Susan. Go ahead. Give it a whirl. You'll do fine," he said, with frequent pauses for breath. The test was a written one, the next date for it some six months ahead.

Six months was too long for Hank Beckett. I came home one Sunday morning after an absence of not much over half an hour and found him dead. One horrified look sent me running, frantic, for help. Later, I couldn't remember what I had seen. I mean, I really couldn't. Not for a very long time.

Well, I went ahead and took the examination, and passed it, and then simply went on where I was. It was home. I had

13

never lived anywhere else. Besides, I was Beckett's, of Belmont.

The Fosters were a tremendous help. Joe Foster was available. I never invaded a board meeting, but I knew that I could, and the only time I had to sue, to collect on two mahogany slipper chairs and a late Sheraton sideboard, Joe sicked his firm's high-priced legal talent onto the trail and picked up the tab for the service.

"I can pay my own way, you do too much."

Joe Foster held up a restraining hand. "Hank Beckett was my friend," he said quietly. "I'll do what I can for his daughter."

Courtesy uncle on the way to becoming Father Joe, except that I was too old by then to call him "uncle." Even Margaret did her best, although she was not the stuff of courtesy aunts. Still, she was punctilious with dinner invitations once or twice a month, and for Margaret that represented an effort. By the time I knew her, she was a wispy, fragile woman who wanted it understood that she didn't expect anyone to go out of his way for her benefit, when all she wanted was her own way.

Hearty, ruddy Joe Foster adored her, and when she died of pneumonia about two months after Hank, Joe was disconsolate. I almost put *pneumonia* in quotes. Joe called it that. Margaret had languished in bed with a cold for a few days, getting up only when Joe was home; then she would not be parted from him. There was a touching note of pride in Joe Foster's voice when he told me about it after she died. Usually, it was Joe who had clung, psychologically, to Margaret.

"Maybe she had some sort of—of premonition, Susan, and wanted to spend her last hours with me." Desperate, groping hope. I had no answer to give him.

She felt well enough her last day to spread one of those late afternoon, female-type tea parties—a kind of party that she loved and did very well. Tea and coffee, and petits fours and cookies and tiny sandwiches, all the food ordered in from

14

a caterer and all guaranteed to spoil everybody's dinner. I was there, along with Cora Whitney (we both helped pour), the Misses Sanders from the other end of Belmont, and a dozen or so of Margaret's socialite friends with time on their hands. Some of them took a turn behind the tea- or coffeepot when Margaret flattered them prettily about how gracious they were to do it.

Maybe Joe was right, though. Maybe it was pneumonia. After the party—we all left early because we could see her tiring—Margaret lay down for a nap and fell into a sleep from which she could not be wakened. Early that night she died.

"Walking pneumonia," Joe said in a numb tone. "I told her." He turned a stunned gaze on me. "Why wouldn't she go to the hospital? I told her to be careful. You know she was never strong. Why?" Total, blank bewilderment. "Why?"

I had no answer for him. All I knew—all Belmont knew— was that Margaret Foster suddenly, surprisingly, was dead. Shocking, but there it was.

After a time Joe left off asking his pathetic "Why?" It was my turn to be the rallying force. I called Joe at the office every now and then—he went back to work almost immediately—and went to see him every week without fail. And sold him antiques.

The man would buy anything, provided only that it was old. It was how he filled his time after hours, as patron of every flea market and antique shop within a fifty-mile radius. We talked antiques when I went to see him, and he showed me his latest finds, one piece at a time. Since one acquisition consisted of fifty-seven silver souvenir spoons—well, we got a lot of mileage out of those spoons.

"He's ga-ga," Betty said one day upon learning about a certain bedstead and bureau, when she dropped in at Beckett's on her lunch hour. She was somebody's executive secretary in an office not too far from Belmont. Betty had progressed from a twenty pounds overweight lump in ill-

15

chosen bulky sweaters, with straight black hair hanging halfway down her back to slim chic in a modish French gray suit that fit where it should. Now all that black hair was coiled into a disciplined chignon. Betty was an eyeful, and knew it.

"Somebody out to do something," she said, examining the toe of her black lizard skin pump.

Joe Foster wasn't ga-ga, just lonely.

Betty moved out soon after Margaret died, when Joe began to hit his stride on collecting. "The place gives me the creeps," she said.

After awhile Ray couldn't stand it either and he moved out, too.

Joe Foster saw them both go with no hard feelings. Their leaving netted him more space to fill. It also left him alone in the house. Ray was pretty good about going to see his father, although there was never the rapport between them that had existed between Ray and his mother. Betty went less often, which I thought rather too bad of her, for Joe Foster had given her a home for several years. Still, there it was.

Ray's and Betty's eyes rested on me, figuratively speaking, in tacit assumption that I would take up the slack.

"You know how to talk to him," said Ray in the only overt recognition ever given to Joe Foster's loneliness.

So I did all I could, and didn't begrudge the time. Joe Foster had done a lot for me, too.

But we never talked about the Chippendale highboy. In the nearly nine years that I called regularly on Joe Foster, and went to shows and auctions with him, and admired what he bought, or wrangled with him fruitlessly when he got took, which happened about every three months—during all that time the highboy was never once mentioned and I never saw it.

There was no reason for Joe to hark back to it. I was the one who was intermittently haunted by Hank's blunder. My ears, not (I was confident) Joe Foster's, rang to a silent *Hank, how could you?* until the inner monitors switched off the sound.

As time went on I grew ever more reluctant to challenge that inner, anguished query. The monitors snapped to red alert in the instant to stifle the plea. I had learned just how easy it was to fool Joe Foster; for with all his exposure to antiques and all the money that he spent on them, he never developed much of an eye for the subtle differences that made one better than another. Joe Foster was the perfect C in the equation.

In spite of myself, my inner cry to Hank shifted a bit in meaning as there grew, behind it and still deeper, a possibility that I preferred not to examine. And so I forbore to press Joe about the highboy.

Now, Joe Foster was dead, with no more chance to ask him anything, even if I had the courage.

2

HARD BEHIND CORA Whitney's visit, Ray phoned. "The hospital called. I'll pick you up."

I refused to go all black and funereal. This was the season for daffodils, and Joe Foster, bless him, was fond of them. "Them and roses I can recognize," he said, every spring. I zipped myself into a pale yellow dress, passed a comb through my hair, and made motions with a lipstick, just finishing when Ray arrived.

Ray Foster is what many people have in mind when they think of Anglo-Saxon: a shock of hair the color of ripe wheat and very blue eyes. He took his coloring from Margaret and his stature from Joe. Ray stood a head taller than most other men on the street, and kept all those inches in trim by thrice-weekly swimming. And dancing. We still went, often. Our steps just fit.

"You ready to go?"

"Soon as I close up shop." I hung the "Closed" sign on the door and locked it, not bothering about a shop-sitter, although we're good along Belmont about keeping an eye on each other's premises when need arises. Tuesday mornings were slow anyway.

Ray handed me briskly across the sidewalk to the car parked illegally at the curb. We didn't talk much on the way to the hospital. In the face of death there never seems to be anything to say.

"I wish I'd gone to see him yesterday," Ray said at one point. "I was going, but then things happened."

"Well—Monday. Things do." To myself, I speculated that

Ray had been busy with the deal he had been putting together recently. After several years of job-hopping, looking for the one that suited him, he had more or less settled in some sort of loose arrangement with a smallish company that dealt in electronic components and also did some servicing, I think, in which his business management talents were coupled with someone else's engineering savvy.

He never talked much about his business life to me. The Foster men didn't talk to their women that way. They wanted them as Little Women to their Strong Protectors. It was the one serious point of disagreement between Ray and me. I told myself it was why I was still single at twenty-seven: he wanted me to close the shop and just be Mrs. Ray Foster.

"You don't want to work after we're married, you won't have to work. It's all right for now, sweetheart, but I'll be set in a few years and then you won't want to work. Let me take care of you."

When Ray's tone softened and he called me sweetheart, all doubts disappeared. *Of course* Lancelot would take care of his own! *Certainly* I wanted to be protected by Ray! Still . . . I was Beckett's, of Belmont. Hank and I had started the shop together. I worked hard after he was gone to build it. I loved it and was proud of it. Even so, I'd have married Ray a dozen times and taken our chances on working out our differences on the shop. I was sure he'd come around to my side, once we were married. But Ray liked to do things in his own time. Having a wife meant supporting her as he thought fit. Lancelot. I respected him for it.

And he was coming closer. For the last year and a half Ray had been somewhat more than an employee but not quite a partner. Now they were incorporating and he had a chance to buy in. I had a hunch that Joe Foster was putting up the money, but whether he had actually done so . . .

At the hospital we were passed through channels until we wound up with one of the floor nurses who could release Joe's personal belongings to us. Mrs. Kern's identity was revealed by her dog tag. Her eyes look enormous in her thin face, and she had a nose like a stiletto.

"How did he go? Slip away in his sleep?" Ray asked her as we stood around the empty bed, already stripped and anonymous.

Mrs. Kern shook her head. "Not that one," she said. "He died game. Trying to say something," she added reflectively.

"Say something!" Ray echoed. "He tried to speak?"

"They do, sometimes," said Mrs. Kerns, chillingly matter-of-fact about the universal desire to be heard.

"Well, but—could you understand it?"

"Part of it. He said 'Tell.' Took several tries, but that was plain. But then he trailed off in a kind of hissing sound, not a word, you understand." The voice was still detached, but the enormous eyes were kind. "At the end he hissed again and there was a long 'oo-oo-o.' That may not have been part of it."

"Well—thank you for telling us," Ray said, after a moment.

Ray appeared as much preoccupied as sad, as we made our way back to the car, not noticing the attention that followed his progress out of the hospital. Ray attracted female attention wherever he went, and the only thing that kept him from being hopelessly spoiled was the two years he had spent in Europe. Joe called it bumming around, making a joke of how much Ray was missed, but in fact Ray was going to college in Switzerland. He had finished his sophomore year when his mother saw to it that he took advantage of some sort of exchange program. I used to wonder how Margaret made an assessment of the superiority of Swiss universities. Joe gave in, as he generally did. Margaret was not one to see reason when she had set her heart on something. Ray had been gone six months when his mother died. Ray came home for her funeral, of course, and went back almost immediately.

I saw him go with secret tears and filled the time while he was gone with adoring letters three times a week that I signed

"All my love." After Hank died, there was no one else to give love to. Ray answered at intervals, when he could—I understood how busy he was—calling me his sweetheart and urging me to "keep your letters coming. They mean a great deal to me." I kept them coming.

Ray followed me into the shop, muttering under his breath, sat in a beat-up Morris chair that I hadn't got around to repairing, and turned unfocused, very blue eyes on me.

Then his eyes brightened. "Got it!" he yelped. "Listen! Tell s-s-s-s-oo-oo-o—tell Susan!" he interpreted on a note of triumph.

Well—yes. I reached the same conclusion on the way home, but—tell Susan what? What had Joe Foster to say to me that he hadn't said repeatedly? Adopting Ray's cause as his own, Joe Foster had promoted marriage between Ray and me by every device of ballyhoo he could summon to hand or tongue. I wanted the urgency to come from Ray.

"You know what was on his mind," Ray pursued soberly. "On mine, too."

I nodded. "I suppose so."

Ray Foster stood up and reached for me purposefully. "We can be married in about three months, wouldn't you say? There's no point in waiting longer, when it was Dad's dearest wish as well as mine."

I had feared he would never say it. Now, perversely, my mind was on something else. "Whoa! Not so fast."

As Ray put his arms around me, I got one hand flat against his chest and unloosed a shove that sat him back in the Morris chair with a thump.

"I can't marry you in three months, Ray. A girl wants to set her own date and have time, when it's set, to—to get ready."

From the depths of the Morris chair Ray gazed up at me in some perplexity.

"What'd I do wrong?" he said, and then, unerringly,

"something's on your mind, Susan, what's the trouble?"

Secretly, I knew what ailed me. In spite of myself I had peeked at the contents of the hidden closet, and having peeked, knew I would never get that door slammed and safely barred without a tussle.

"I wish—" I almost stopped there, but the words dragged out—"wish I'd talked with Joe about the Chippendale highboy, asked him about it, or something."

"Highboy? Chippendale?"

"Yes," reluctantly, "one that Joe bought."

Ray gave me a patient look. "Dad bought tons of stuff, Susan. I wouldn't be surprised," said Ray, "if Dad had half a dozen highboys here and there." He made them sound like piggy banks.

"Chippendale?"

He shrugged. "Who knows? What about it?"

I had no wish to put false notions into Ray's head. Yet there was no way to say identifying words without saying them. "This highboy is one that Hank appraised for Joe before he bought it."

No pennies dropped for Ray. "Well, Hank did a lot of that, as I recall, before his heart went back on him."

Yes, it had been his profession, that was all, not some pastime for a rainy Sunday.

"You act like you expect me to remember," Ray prodded. "Be reasonable, Susan. Whatever you're talking about goes back—what? Hank's been dead six or seven years, so at least that long ago—"

"Ten years, Hank's been dead ten years."

"As long as that? Long time. Out with it, honey. I wouldn't remember a thing about a carload of what-do-you-call-'ems—highboys—when I'm not interested in old stuff."

"That highboy wasn't just old stuff. It was a fine antique and Hank so appraised it. Only, when it was put on display after Joe bought it, it—well, it wasn't. So everybody said."

"So." Ray shrugged. "Hank called it wrong." He studied

23

my face, then continued in a gentle tone freighted with reason. "There are only two possibilities. One, Hank made a mistake. So what? Everyone does."

I had been telling myself that for a decade.

"Or else Hank fudged a bit," Ray said in that same voice of sweet reason. "Again, Susan—so what?"

I had trouble getting my voice going. It came out a notch higher than usual. "Hank Beckett was not a crook!"

"Now, Susan, I never said he was."

"The hell you didn't! You just finished saying so!"

Ray studied my face again for storm warnings. "Okay, maybe I didn't say it quite right."

"Maybe you didn't," I said through my teeth, "maybe you just didn't. Maybe you should say exactly what you mean."

Ray sighed. "All I'm trying to say is, it was a long time ago. Ten years, you said. They're all dead, everybody who had anything to do with it. How can any of them be helped now by anything you or I can do? What difference can it make—to them?" His tone took on the exaggerated patience of a teacher explaining to pupils who are nice kids all, but a little dim.

"Go on," I said, "I'm listening."

"That's all," Ray said, surprise in his voice. He waited a moment, then went on with more assurance. "When we're married, sweetheart, I think we'll dispose of all that stuff Dad piled up."

"I'd like a look at—things beforehand, before anything is sold." Why the notion surfaced just then, I couldn't have said, but all at once I wanted to see that highboy that had stood in the shadows of my life for ten years. What I thought it might reveal to me that it hadn't already disclosed to experts—I had no idea.

"Why?" And then, "Oh—stock, you mean, for the shop? Oh, I don't think so, Susan, you won't need the shop once we're married. You don't think"—he assumed a playful tone—"I'd let my wife work, do you?"

24

"Stick to the point, Ray. I'm talking about the highboy."

He sighed. "Leave it be, Susan. This constant harking back is—it's morbid."

"Morbid or not, I'd like to see it."

"But what do you think you'd gain?"

"Probably not much," I said with unwilling honesty. "Probably nothing. It's just—I'd like to see it."

Ray loosed a heavier sigh. "No, Susan. No. My dear, you're building a mountain. Look. So this highboy—Chippendale?—yes, wasn't all it was cracked up to be. All right. If Hank goofed—well, that's no crime. Or if he didn't—what if he did inflate his estimate a bit—who was harmed? Dad could afford the dollars. He got his money's worth, Susan, out of thinking the damned thing was something special. Nobody was cheated, so what's the difference?"

I held my voice down. "The difference is whether Hank Beckett was a—an incompetent fool or a crook. That's all. And you do surprise me, Ray, how ready you are to believe he was crooked!"

"I haven't said I believe he was crooked," Ray howled. "I've said I don't know. I've said it's an open question, leave it open."

"Leave it open?" I raged. "Oh, you are generous! You don't know that Hank cheated, but you'll agree that he might have!"

"Now, Susan—"

"Don't you Susan me! Damn you, Ray, you *knew* Hank. You knew what he was and what he stood for. There shouldn't *be* any question in your mind, open or closed."

"No, there shouldn't," he agreed readily and more calmly. Ray Foster never lost his cool for long. "But people *do* do things, Susan, you wouldn't expect them to do. You know that."

"Not Hank Beckett."

Ray shook his head in sober admonition. "You can believe that all you want, my darling, but you can't prove it, Susan.

That's why I say, leave it. Hank's dead, it can't make any difference to him. Let it go. Concentrate on building your own life."

"With you," I grated, "beginning in three months."

"Why, yes, of course," Ray said simply.

I stared at him for the second it took me to blow up. "Not on your tintype! You listen to me, Ray Foster, I'm not marrying you in three months or any other time—"

"Now, Susan, you don't mean that."

"The hell I don't mean it," I raved, fortissimo. "I'll be busy three months from now, or forever—I'll prove it, prove Hank was no cheat, prove it 'til you gag on your open questions! You—you—" I left off screaming at him to draw breath and choose among several epithets jostling for utterance.

Into the breach Ray Foster, with the air of running up a white flag, injected a cautious "How?"

It was the wrong question. "I don't know," I snarled, loosing a fresh volley. "I don't know. But I'll do it."

The little woman myth dies hard. "Now calm down, dear. You're getting a little extravagant with your claims."

"Out of my shop, damn you, get going! You're in the way."

"Well, really, Susan—"

"Out! I'm busy."

Ray got to his feet, wearing dignity like a halo. "All right, dear. I'll call you later when you're not upset."

Ray's peroration was all but lost in the admiring "Wow!" that swung both our heads toward the girl standing in the doorway.

"That was sure some war whoop," she observed in the same admiring tone, as she stepped inside the shop and swung the door shut behind her. "Peter sent me over to count the bodies. He said you're getting pretty loud."

Dagmar Thornton never shortened "Peter" to "Pete," as did the rest of Belmont Street. This was a leftover from childhood, when she invested the name with an unspoken

26

"Saint" preceding it, as full-blown a case of hero worship by little sister for big brother as I ever encountered.

She was barely twenty-one and possessed of the most ravishing peaches-and-cream coloring ever seen off a candy box. She appeared younger, partly from contrast with Pete's thirty-three years, but more because of the way she pursued her own train of thought despite what went on around her, conveying an impression of being, faintly, elsewhere. For a time after Dagmar and I got acquainted, I wondered what she thought about when she wasn't thinking about what she was doing, but as I knew her better, I realized that was an injustice. Dagmar accomplished what she undertook with commendable efficiency. It was merely that the leftover portion of her mind, so to speak, might or might not intersect yours during any given meeting.

The childish quality of her absentmindedness was enhanced by the unfocused vagueness of her glance. When talking with Dagmar, you were apt to find yourself raising your voice at intervals to exclaim, "Dagmar!" to which she unfailingly replied with perfect good nature, "Hm-m-m? I'm listening." Ten minutes later, perhaps—or two weeks later—she would emit, with a transparent and sometimes embarrassing truthfulness, some answer or comment proving she had indeed been listening more intently than you had credited her with.

Dagmar Thornton coupled the large generosity of judgment and uncritically friendly acceptance of a puppy. Did you need a shop-sitter in a hurry for an indefinite interval? Had you a finicky errand? Dagmar Thornton was your girl. Belmont Street loved her and called on her freely.

"Were you going anywhere in particular?" she asked, turning to Ray.

"Huh?" Ordinary normal quickness of wit wasn't sufficient to follow Dagmar's mental arabesques.

"Well, Susan said you were leaving and I just wondered," she explained patiently. Dagmar was used to explaining what

27

she meant. Even as she spoke, she had produced a list and was consulting it closely.

"Er—I wasn't going right away." Ray essayed a feeble diversion, wary eyes on the list.

"Oh, yes, you are," I cut in without mercy.

"You see?" Dagmar beamed. "So I thought you could take me—" and she reeled off four divergent points of destination.

Man fashion, Ray Foster knew when he was outgeneraled. "Oh, all right," he yielded with poor grace.

Dagmar took no notice. "Fine! You're a big help."

As they went out she turned back to ask, "Did you mean that, Susan, about not marrying him?"

"I never meant anything more."

"Oh. Well, then, maybe I'll marry him instead. We'll see." She eyed Ray as one might inspect a chair frame for structural flaws.

Ray followed her from the shop with a glazed expression.

It was funny, but it wasn't funny, reminding me that I had said too much, too hastily. I couldn't bring off this—this ultimatum alone, yet where could I go for help? Who was there to ask? How, at the remove of a decade could I hope to tease apart the threads that knotted up the past? Hank was dead—gone—beyond reach. Joe Foster was dead—dead. The street itself—where was the Belmont I had known all my life? Gone. Dead. Changed beyond recall.

I flopped into the Morris chair vacated by Ray and howled, crying as I had not wept for years. I thought of the monstrous injustice life had dealt to Hank, and I wept over that. I had been unable to cry when he died, all my tears turning inward. New grief for a dead friend linked hands with the old, and I wept for that. A spring in the Morris chair chose that moment to cast off all ties with a muffled *spon-n-n-g!* that brought me up standing, before I flopped back down and wept the harder about the spring. I thought of my blasted romance—Lancelot, come back!—I thought of lasting

28

spinsterhood—what chance has a girl to meet eligible men when she spends her life rooting through the attics of the doddering?—and wept, in noisy, hiccuping sobs. I wept as long as tears could flow, and when I finally stopped, I felt no better. For at bottom, beneath all else, I wept because I dared not fail. If I began, I must see it through.

If. I didn't really have to begin. Did I? I could back away—take Ray's advice—leave it alone. I could phone him—later, in the evening—and crawl a little bit. Couldn't I? It wouldn't take much of a show of proper humility to regain lost ground. Everything would be just as it was. Wouldn't it? Ray wouldn't take my phoning him as an exhibition of groveling. I knew that would never occur to him. He'd call it Susan Coming to Her Senses. He'd be very kind and the whole sorry episode would be over in a few minutes. This evening. The sensible course.

I sat up and blew my nose and mopped my eyes, and said, "So that's that."

My eyes met their dim reflection in a windowpane.

"My God, you're a mess," I told the swollen-eyed, raw-nosed ruin seen in the transitory mirror.

My heart sank, as the reflected eyes touched mine and slid away from the meeting. All Ray's homilies about the dead not caring left out one vital fact. I wasn't dead and I cared. If I didn't want to spend my life avoiding my own eyes in mirrors, I had to act. A recurrence of the weeps threatened my precarious composure, bringing me uncertainly to my feet. I tottered in search of a washcloth wrung from cold water and held it against my eyes, muttering to myself as I did so.

"Dammit, Joe, Belmont'll never be the same without you," and then, still chewing on my dry stick, "How'm I going to start?" I groped for a renewal of the cold cloth. "I'll go talk to Pete," I decided when at length I finished mopping up. "I'll go pick his brain for ideas. If he'll let me."

3

ANTIQUE DEALERS ARE a competitive crew. They're also gossipy and gregarious, and they know without anyone's needing to say so that everybody's business improves when a number of them locate near each other, unlike gas stations and grocery stores, a seeming anomaly explained by the habits of the customers.

A vast and thriving mercantile exchange in antiques has been erected on the unspoken premise that need has very little to do with the transaction. No one *needs* fifty-seven milk cans painted over with pansies, or a single wastebasket made from an elephant's foot. No one needs a Heppelwhite sofa of indifferent line, loose in all its joints and shedding stuffing and springs. I sold one last week in "as is" condition. During forty minutes of bargaining need was never once mentioned.

More than that, the buyer of antiques very often doesn't know what he wants until he runs across it. The search is all, which leads to the public's engaging custom of donning old clothes, rehearsing the careful tale of poverty, and sallying forth. They contemplate a happy, grimy day of prowling from one place to the next. The charades fool no one—

"Crying poor and her with an easy five carats on her fist." The lady neglected to leave her rings at home.

"Any guy with a watch like that doesn't wear worn-out jeans because he *has* to."

It's all a game in which antique dealers are happy to play their part.

Most of us along Belmont have our specialties. Beckett's

deals chiefly in furniture, eighteenth century American for choice, but most of the best stuff that belongs in a museum is already in a museum somewhere or locked away in a private collection until another rich eccentric dies. I therefore do a good deal of commissioned searching because I'm presumed to know of the existence and availability and probable price of the best pieces. It's my business to be up on what's in the museums (which aren't above selling) and what's in private collections. Rich eccentrics sometimes show off their treasures in confidential viewings. Not all eccentrics, of course. There's a certain Abby Granger right here in the city, of great age and enormous wealth. One affirmative peep from Abby would bring dealers baying a hot trail from all over the country. Abby Granger has preserved her reticence intact for sixty years.

Well, that's my specialty—eighteenth-century American. I handle earlier stuff, as well as English and French goods, but not much Victoriana, leaving that for the specialist across the street and down a block. More exactly, such Victorian furniture as comes into my hands I sell to him, for a significant part of a shop's receipts comes from sales to other dealers.

In like fashion, there are dealers along Belmont in glassware, china and porcelain objects, antique jewelry, silver (very dignified, "Belmont Antique Silver"), copper, brass, woodenware, pewter, and clocks. Also Mason canning jars, Shirley Temple mugs, Nancy Drew mysteries (the binding makes the difference), battered picture frames, and old Coca-Cola signs ("The Fleatique," selling "junque").

And then there's Pete Thornton with "Stuff and Things." If an object once had moving parts, Pete Thornton is likely to have dealt in it either in toto or piece by piece, except clocks and watches.

"Don't be a snob, Susan," Pete had said, grinning, when Miss Seventeen-knows-it-all snooted one of his early displays of hubcaps and hood ornaments. "You know they're antique, you just won't admit it."

I drew breath for combat, when Hank's tired, breathy voice intervened. "He's right, Susan. Cars become antiques legally in twenty-five years."

Pete Thornton always puts me in mind of Jiminy Cricket. Same oval head. Pete's chin is a little narrow for perfect symmetry, his features more irregularly bony than Jiminy's but the general shape is the same, while his shining smooth cap of deep brown hair irresistibly suggests Jiminy's sometimes iridescent brown shell. Likewise, the same skinny arms and legs and somewhat jerky movement, and not least a similar academic interest in a well-turned leg. In Jiminy Cricket's same jaunty manner, Pete Thornton frequently uses a cane, although not as often now as when he and Dagmar first came to Belmont Street. Pete Thornton limped noticeably then. The cane never left his side. War-weary and cynical, a veteran of Vietnam, he was twenty-three, to Dagmar's knobby-kneed eleven. He left a foot in the jungles.

"He came home and said we'd better stick together 'cause neither of us had anyone else to live with," Dagmar told me.

"Home from Vietnam?"

"Uh-huh. Peter cashed his insurance so's to start 'Stuff and Things,' said it'd give him a good sideline view of the rat race. What's a rat race?"

"Sort of like a treadmill. Nobody can stop running and nobody can get off, either."

"Oh." Dagmar considered. "I guess that's right."

"What brought you to Belmont Street?"

"Don't you like having us here?"

"I love you dearly. I only wondered what made you decide on Belmont."

"I don't know," Dagmar said with a child's indifference. "Peter said 'Stuff and Things' gives him a good chance to think. Peter thinks a lot." There was simple pride in her tone, as one reporting mastery of a difficult trick.

Dagmar's artless revelations continued by dribs and drabs.

"What's a Dear John?" she asked the third time I saw her.

"A Dear John?"

"Uh-huh. Peter said someone sent him a Dear John while he was off fighting. He said he left it in the jungle along with his foot."

"Oh. Well, a Dear John is a—a kind of letter. People write them to say they like someone else better."

"That's mean," Dagmar announced, after due reflection.

Two days later she continued the discussion. "Peter felt real bad about the Dear John—mad, too—he said he wasn't going to get burned twice for any female alive."

Ten days after that she added, "Peter feels better about the Dear John now." Dagmar never abandoned a subject until she had exhausted its possibilities. "He sounded surprised when he said so. Why would feeling better surprise anyone, Susan?" She added, naively, "Peter says you're awfully pretty."

But that time she was unlucky. Pete caught her in midflight and led her home—the end of her sentence trailed back over her shoulder—promising in a pleasant tone to skin her with a dull knife if she ever unbuttoned her lip again. He may have exhibited the knife, but nothing could silence Dagmar completely.

After a time the Thorntons became fixtures of Belmont, so that my small itch of curiosity subsided, which was just as well, because they lived next door for nearly five months before Pete mentioned that they hailed originally from Connecticut. Pete elevated the concept of minding his own business to the status of a high and holy calling. To elicit from Pete any comment about himself called for circumstances beyond the ordinary.

Hank's obituary freed the tidbit about Connecticut at the obligatory feast that follows a funeral.

34

"Didn't know you were from Connecticut, too," he offered, thrusting a coffee cup into my hand.

"Not me. Just Hank," and we talked about origins for a few minutes, Pete musing aloud for my benefit with the same detached interest he bestowed on everything.

"Knew a guy once from the Gobi Desert. Fact. That's what he put on the line for place of birth."

"Imagine trying to get a birth certificate."

"No trouble at all," Pete assured me, and went on about the provisions governing vital statistics of citizens born in remote places.

Hank Beckett and Pete Thornton took to each other very near the beginning of the few months that their lives overlapped. I thought their initial meeting ground was their mutual awareness of disability. Hank didn't speak of his damaged, gallantly laboring heart, while Pete acknowledged his prosthetic foot one time only, when it developed an embarrassing squeak that could not be overlooked.

"Sorry, sir," Pete said, avoiding all eyes, "I'm really not carrying a litter of mice around with me."

"Do you want a screwdriver or a bit of oil?" Hank inquired with a directness that was the essence of tact.

"Both, I expect."

Hank directed me to fetch them and then banished me from the scene. "Susan! Get out. Go somewhere else for a while."

Pete came over nearly every day when Hank got home from the hospital. And when I came home that last day and found Hank, I ran to Pete Thornton for help.

We traded help through the years, chiefly his lending a hand when there was no substitute for muscle. In return, the first two or three years I helped him identify bits and pieces of larger wholes before he sold them.

"What the hell is it?" he said one day as he brandished a

35

wooden rod with wooden cross members attached to one end, each arm of the cross with a hole drilled in it near its outer end.

Then, without warning he dropped the rod, said, "Oh, God damn it, Susan," wrapped both arms around me and kissed me, hard.

I was too startled to squirm.

After awhile he raised his head and glared at me. "All right, don't look so scared."

"I'm not scared," I said, freeing myself with the dignity of affronted seventeen-plus, "but I am engaged. Practically engaged."

"Yeah," on a savage note, "to Ray Foster. You've told me. Good looking. Rich. Whole. No girl wants a chopped off cripple."

"Why, it isn't that at all," I explained carefully, "it's just that I'm in love with Ray. I've always been in love with him."

"Yeah." Savagery faded from his voice and eyes. "Okay, toots," he said then, and summoned a smile. "Okay. You might even grow up someday." Then he kissed me again, a chaste, brotherly peck on the cheek, picked up the wooden rod, and said, "Now about this whatsit?"

"It's an old-time churn dasher for making butter."

"Oh, well, somebody can use it planting tulips." To my incredulous stare, he explained, "For firming the soil."

Pete was a quick study. Within six months of opening Stuff and Things he had soaked up the overriding principle of selling antiques. Never mind what the widget was used for when new. The demand for buggy whips today *as buggy whips* is negligible. The real question is what can the customer be persuaded to do with a widget now? Collect it. Two of anything counts as a collection. From there on, they're off and running.

The Fosters' Chippendale highboy was a different matter altogether. I had no reason to think Hank ever discussed the incident with Pete, and little expectation that Pete would remember, highboys being outside his territory. But I had to talk to someone.

I gave a final inspection to my face, wrung out the washcloth and hung it up, blew my nose once more, and dabbed on lipstick.

Pete was lounging in a barber's chair (one of five filling up the front of the store) and leafing through the shop manual of a 1931 V-16 Cadillac.

"Hi, Susan." Pete's quick glance took in my bedraggled appearance. He withheld comment, gesturing expansively instead toward the remaining four chairs.

"What do you think of 'em? Go ahead, try one, very comfortable. Bought 'em yesterday at auction. Contents of a barber shop went up. I've got the shoe shine stands here somewhere. They'll be great in somebody's hall closet for drying overshoes."

"Yes, I'm sure. Pete—"

"Yesterday was a good day," Pete interrupted, flourishing the shop manual. "Found this in a box lot at the same auction. Must've been money in barbering. Or maybe the guy read 'em like comic books."

He was giving me a chance to change my mind. Pete has been heard to say that most burning confidences are regretted later on—or should be. So when Pete sees words jostling for utterance, he looses a countering barrage allowing time for unlucky impulses to subside.

"They sure don't build 'em like they used to," he flowed on. "Listen to this!" Pete dived into the manual and read to me the details about uncoupling the drive train of a 1931 V-16 Cadillac.

"Yes, yes," I said with scant attention. "Pete—"

"And on page thirty-eight—"

"Pete! Pay attention!"

"All right." He sighed and put down the manual.

"Pete, did Hank—did Hank ever talk to you about a

Chippendale highboy he appraised for the Fosters?

"Joe Foster died this morning, didn't he? Cora told us," he added unnecessarily, giving me a thoughtful look. "Is that what you were yelling about? Incidentally, what happened to Dagmar?"

"She drafted Ray to chauffeur."

"Oh. Poor devil."

"Poor devil nothing," I returned with some heat. "Did he? Hank? Mention it, that you remember?"

Pete looked away from me into the past. "He might have," he said after an interval. "What's with the highboy?"

It was my turn to scan the past. Hank had not talked of the highboy directly, yet he "might have" mentioned it, with such emphasis that Pete remembered after ten years.

"What did he say, Pete?"

"What about the highboy?"

I gave him a terse summary.

Pete retired into thought, and as he reflected, his face changed. "That must have been it," he said in a neutral tone. "I never knew all that before."

"So?"

"There'd been a story in the paper about some guy tried to burgle his own house—phony insurance claim, I suppose, I've forgotten—anyway, we were talking about the dumb things people do. And after awhile I said the dumbest thing I'd done so far was to get too close to the bang. Hank said that was just bad luck, and anyway a foot could be replaced, sort of." Pete broke off and looked at me with pity in his eyes. "You're not going to like this, Susan."

"Go on. What came after that?"

"Well," Pete returned to his story, "I thought he was talking to himself more than me. Because then he said some things couldn't be put back, not approximately, not any way. Then he laughed, like someone seeing the point of an unfunny joke. And then he said—and then he *was* talking to himself—'and of course we needed money.'"

38

"Those were his exact words?" I asked dully.

"That's what he said, Susan," Pete said gently. "I told you you wouldn't like it."

I bestirred myself. "Pete, tell me something else. When you and Dagmar moved to Belmont, did you hear anything said about Hank and the highboy?"

Pete took his time in answering. "Not so much that anybody talked about him to me—we were new, then—as, well—I thought he was in trouble. More trouble than a bum ticker."

"I—see."

"No." Pete was thoughtful. "I don't think you do. Okay, so I thought maybe the poor devil had tried a hustle and been unlucky with it."

"Hank never did—"

"Don't yell at me, toots. All right, let's say I wondered."

I got a tight grip on my voice. "Hank Beckett was no hustler, and I'll prove it to you, too!"

"Fine. Now I'll tell you something else. I liked Hank anyway. Didn't matter what he might have done or not done. He didn't have to be God. You talk about proof. Great. But what about you, Susan?" Pete said, gentleness again in his tone, "would you love him—his memory—as much if your proof turned out the other way?"

There it was, laid out on a tray, the secret fear I had dodged for ten years. "I don't know, Pete," I said wretchedly.

Pete Thornton was very kind. "Then I think you'd better prove—whatever can be proved—and find out. Stop running scared."

Sitting there in one of Pete's old pump-up barber chairs, I really tried to imagine Hank Beckett as a cheat, a kind of thief.

"Why would he, Pete?" There was the sticking point.

Pete Thornton shrugged. "Sometimes there isn't much of a why, Susan. Sometimes a guy just gets tired of always being the good guy."

I shook my head. "Not Hank. He didn't go around as a good guy because of what he'd get out of it."

"All right, maybe he got too curious about how would it feel to do this or that, and found out too late there was no going back. That happens."

Again, stubbornly, I shook my head. "Not Hank. You're describing someone with no imagination who's got to live his consequences because he can't picture them beforehand. That wasn't Hank."

"Okay." Pete grinned. "Then he's innocent. You're right. Go to it, Susan—sic 'em—and the Lord go with you."

"How?"

Pete shook his head. "Sorry. Don't know. Can't help you there."

"But where do I start?"

"Go back over the ground—"

"Do you think I haven't done that? The first year after Hank died I spent every spare minute with it."

"It?"

"Hank's notebook. He kept a—a journal, I guess you'd call it. A notebook. Several. Fifteen."

"What were they, annuals, one per year?"

"No, just notebooks. Not even all alike. Hank used one until it was filled up and then got another. They're no help, Pete. You see, Hank used them to jog his memory. To anyone else they don't mean anything—or too much."

"How so, Susan?"

"Hank had a prodigious memory for furniture. He didn't only see desks or beds, he saw an individual desk or bed. Once he'd gone over a piece, he'd recognize it if he ever saw it again. If he didn't see it, he still remembered it. 'Oh, yes,' I've heard him say, 'the Queen Anne armchair with gooseneck arms, very weak curvature, structurally weak, of course. There'd been repairs.' And so on, Pete, talking about a chair he'd seen once, eight or nine years before then. Well, what went into his notebooks was reminders."

40

"Oh—ow," said Pete in the tone of one who now saw clearly.

"Ow's the word."

Pete ran a hand through his hair a little wildly. "Yeah. But when he made a what-do-you-call-it when he'd appraised something—"

"His report."

"—yeah, well, didn't he do it in *writing*? And keep a copy?"

I couldn't help smiling at the naked incredulity in Pete Thornton's voice. When he was alive, Hank Beckett often evoked that reaction.

"Not always, Pete. He did, if the client wanted it. And yes, he kept copies. Usually. I caught him skipping every once in awhile and he always said he had his notes. But the Foster highboy was on a different basis. He looked that over for them out of friendship. Hank wouldn't have kept a copy of that transaction, any more than people keep copies of letters to friends. They just don't. No, I think there wasn't anything. Because I looked. There wasn't any."

"Didn't the Fosters ever say anything to clue you?"

I looked back in time for a long interval before I said, slowly, "You hadn't been here long when it started, Pete. Hank got sick right soon after the highboy went sour, and none of us had any time left over to think about it. We were too busy trying to keep him breathing."

"Right soon. Didn't it ever occur to you there might be some connection between that highboy appraisal and his first heart attack?"

"Oh, Pete, what do you take me for? Of course, it did. But I had to give that up, too. Because when people talked about how bad he'd looked—well, he *did* look tired, and he *had* been short of breath sometimes—only we didn't know what it meant."

"Like a bomb waiting to go off."

"Yes. Like that. He was in the hospital thirteen weeks, had another attack there."

"In the hospital." Pete was indignant. "What happened?"

"I don't know. He was doing fine, could begin to have visitors, and they were talking about letting him come home before long, and then—bang. I went to see him that day and he was back in an oxygen tent, and couldn't come home for another six weeks."

"Something must have happened," Pete insisted.

I shook my head. "Nothing except inside his heart, Pete. Because when he did come home—" I stopped.

Pete was looking at me strangely.

"What is it, Pete?" I asked, when he didn't say anything.

"Have you ever—uh, wondered—" Pete was choosing his words—"about your father—dying—then? Right *then*?"

"Why, he had another heart attack—massive. He must have. The doctor came—didn't he? I never could remember."

"Why, you poor kid," Pete said under his breath with another strange glance my way. Then in his normal tone, "Yes, he came, Susan. The doctor came. The damned fool!"

Suddenly, I was back in time, hearing Pete's voice saying those words. They acted just like a switch, setting a reel unrolling in my mind, and I was living again that dreadful Sunday morning.

Hank had been home nine days and improving steadily. He ate his breakfast with a better appetite than he had shown since falling sick.

"You ate it all, Hank!"

"Sure did, kitten. Tasted pretty good, too."

Then I helped him to a chair where he could rest while I changed the bed. We were down to the end of the sheets and pillowcases—I'd have to get the laundry done. I inspected the last pillowcase with a critical eye before slipping it over the pillow. Worn—I held it up to the light—but there weren't any holes. It would do. I drew the sheets taut, proud of my newfound dexterity, replaced the covers, plumped the

42

pillow, and helped Hank back to bed. Half an hour in a chair was enough to tire him. But his color was better.

"Everything okay, Hank?" I bent over him after getting him settled.

"Okay. I'm fine, Susan." Hank lifted a hand to touch my face in a light caress. "I'm just fine."

I covered his hand with my own for a moment before tucking it down at his side, noticing as I did so how thin it was. Thin, but not so desperately transparent as it had been.

"You're getting better, Hank, every day."

"Sure. Sure I am.

"Well, snooze awhile, and you'll feel better yet."

I set the door ajar and left him. I had to get out to a drugstore. We were running low on rubbing alcohol. I looked in on Hank again before I left. He was asleep.

I hurried around to Nineteenth Street where there was a drugstore open early Sunday morning. A cloudy morning with a layer of fog that would burn off later. Belmont Street looked deserted. Belmont sleeps late Sunday in the lull between Saturday's late business and the Sunday rush that will start around two o'clock.

I wasn't gone more than thirty minutes. I let myself into the house, moving quietly as I had learned to do, hung up my coat and put away the alcohol, and then looked in again on Hank.

Then there was no need to be quiet. Hank wasn't fine. Hank was—Hank was dead! Dead—his face all blue! It scarcely looked human. The hand that I had laid at his side was flung up beside his head, palm turned up. The other, palm to the mattress, was thrust out from his side.

Pete says I screamed. I know I ran, to beat a frenzied summons at his door.

"Pete! Pete—Hank's—! He's—! Hurry, Pete! Oh, hurry!"

"Right with you, toots."

He went back with me and had his own look, and turned

me forcibly away from the foreign object with the half-open eyes, the knees drawn up and turned to one side, there in the rumpled bed where Hank had slept, turned me so I could not see the terrible blue face lying askew on the pillow.

Arms tight around me, Pete pressed my face into his shoulder so I couldn't see. "Steady, Susan. Steady."

I didn't cry, but I began shaking and couldn't stop.

He made me go with him to telephone the doctor, and then put me into a chair. I huddled there, shaking—staring—listening—shaking.

Pete went in with the doctor. I could hear their voices in low-pitched, animated discussion.

The doctor's voice rose. "Nonsense, man! Massive coronary. With his history—all the signs consistent with it."

Pete flung out of the room. "The damned fool!"

Mist surged up and receded. I was sitting in Pete's barber chair with him standing over me. "You all right, toots?"

"All right," I said faintly. Collecting myself, I asked in a firmer voice, "What did you mean then? How was the doctor foolish?"

Again Pete chose his words. "Did you strip the bed—well, afterward?"

I nodded.

"Did you notice anything—call it, unusual—about the—the condition of the linen?"

Pete gave me time. "There was a small tear—ragged looking—in the pillowslip."

Pete nodded.

"I put it on clean that morning. It was old, but I thought it would stand a few more washings. Only, it didn't. It got torn."

"I saw it, too. What do you think tore it? It wasn't a clean rip, remember, like when old threads give way. I'll tell you something else, too. That little tear was on the underneath side, Susan, the side away from his head. What do you think tore it?"

44

I shook my head.

"Don't you see?" Soft urgency prodded at me. "It could have been torn if Hank—well, chewed at it?"

Chewed. And the pillow put back, later, except that someone forgot to turn the torn side up, where it might be accounted for, somehow, normally.

"But Pete, are you saying—that someone *killed* Hank?"

Pete's face was grim. "His face—forgive me, Susan—and the way he was lying—they were the face and posture of a man who died fighting. Hank didn't fight very long, Susan." Pete was comforting. "His heart likely did give out before long. But he tried."

I shifted about in my chair. "But you never told me—did you say anything, then, about what you suspected?"

"You're damn right I did. That idiot M.D. wouldn't listen. Next day I told the police. But by then Hank had been moved, and the doctor had signed a death certificate. It was only my word against his, and he was the expert as far as the police were concerned."

There was a silence.

"Why didn't you ever tell me?"

Pete's answer was slow in coming. "You'd have had to know how it was with me then," he said finally. "I couldn't prove anything. And you'd had about all you could stand. You were on the ragged edge."

There was another silence.

"I don't know where to begin. Don't know *what* to begin."

Pete spread his hands. "I can't tell you anything different, Susan, than I've already said. Go back over the ground, and keep going over it 'til you find a piece that doesn't fit."

4

HANK–MURDERED. BY someone who got away with it. It was easy to believe Pete while I listened to him spell it out. Everything fit. All the wrongness in the room that Sunday morning made a pattern. Only—the police hadn't believed him. It was the police, with all their resources and manpower, who solved murders. Murder was their business, and they hadn't been persuaded. Pete himself said he didn't *know*. Besides, ten years ago Pete Thornton was not long home from a shooting war, where he had seen a lot of killing. What more likely than that he'd see violence where there was none? When he aired his suspicion to the doctor, the doctor disagreed. *He* hadn't been in any war. I thought of going again to the police. But Pete went, at the time. The police said no, *at the time*. The police weren't fools.

But Pete was persuaded about the highboy. There was no humor-the-little-woman or soothe-the-doting-daughter in his manner or in his tone. Pete believed in Hank Beckett's honesty because he had known Hank. Yet he hadn't known Hank long enough for his partisanship to be the unthinking bias of a friend. No. Pete let me argue him into Hank's corner because what Hank was had shone forth for Pete to see.

Well, then. Might not others be open to persuasion as well? After all, Joe and Margaret Foster never doubted. Maybe it was a case of everybody tiptoeing around a sick man, nobody bringing up a touchy subject because nobody knew how. All right, trot around to each in turn. Talk to them, sweetly, reasonably, show them how wrong they were.

I played with this euphoric fantasy for an hour or more before I came to my senses. Doubt wouldn't roll over and play dead no matter how much I ran around crying, "Down! Good boy!" This highboy is not as fine as Hank Beckett certified. Hank Beckett would not have made such a mistake. Therefore, Hank Beckett certified falsely. There was the form of doubt, and I didn't have to look further than Ray Foster to know that doubt hung about the name of Beckett like a cloud of gnats.

Nonetheless, I had found my starting point. For when I spun romantic fancies of Susan enlightening the ignorant, I had specific members of the ignorant in mind: Margaret Foster's dinner guests. It all started at that ill-starred party ten years back.

Whoever they were, I wanted to rummage through their mental attics and shake out their moths of memory. Who had been present at Margaret's damnable dinner? How could I frame questions eliciting total recall of disaster until I knew who the witnesses were? There I stuck for three distracting days. It was late Friday evening before I knew how to cut a ten-year-old trail.

First it was Joe's funeral. When, however, under cover of a lengthy prayer, Ray slipped a hand over mine and said, just above a whisper, "Always together, sweetheart, you and I, that's the way it ought to be," he went too far.

"The hell it is!" I shot back in the same half whisper.

Ray took his hand away and finished the service in an affronted silence.

He got over his snit by the next morning and was on the phone, announcing that I should be ready when he came by to pick me up. There was a will to be read. I thought the custom of formally reading a will to panting heirs-expectant had died not long after Dickens. I erred. Joe Foster left a will. Mr. Wyndham proposed to read it.

"Damn it, no, Ray," I said, reduced to profanity the fourth time around. "I've no business there. I'm not family. And I'm not going to be," I forged on, warned by his intake of breath.

Ray let out his breath in an aggrieved sigh and said he guessed he'd have to go alone, then. I said yes, I guessed he would. That afternoon, however, when Betty telephoned, I wondered whether I had erred again in not going.

"Who or what is Eastlake?" she demanded without preamble.

"Well, now it's a style of furniture. Once it was a man's name. Charles Eastlake, and he more or less designed the furniture, and I wish he hadn't. Big, boxy, square stuff with moldings and trims and rosettes and carvings and rows of spindling all laid on with a spatula, and hung about with itsy-bitsy shelves and galleries. Dreadful stuff, most of it."

"Congratulations. You now own Joe's Eastlake chest. Assuming," she added in a disagreeable tone, "he had only one and it can be identified. Also," and now malice was open, "ten thousand in cash. Which takes most of it, I might add. Ray and I get the 'rest and residue' in a seventy-thirty split, seventy to Ray, of course. Mr. Wyndham was very kind in explaining 'rest and residue.'"

I stared at the receiver in dumb disbelief.

"Are you there?" it squawked, irascibility made shrill by the mechanics of sound sent along a wire. "Say something."

"Yes, Betty, I'm here."

"I asked old Wyndham when we'd get ours and he said er-ah that depended on when the estate was settled." Grievance came over the wire with unimpaired fidelity. "Fat lot of help that is, I need money now."

"Don't we all."

"No, I mean, I *need* it."

Betty Foster, to my certain knowledge, owed everybody in town and had ever since the advent of her first credit card. Relations between us were cemented on a firm foundation the first time I refused a small loan.

"I can't do anything about that, Betty, I don't have any money either."

49

"Oh, well, I didn't mean that, exactly," she replied in a tone that said she did mean that, exactly.

"I don't have the ten grand, and I won't have it, probably, for some time, and it won't be ten grand anyway by the time I get it. Whatever's left I have plans for."

"What plans?"

"I'll make some."

"Oh. Well, what I really wondered—do you suppose he left any more?"

"Any more what?"

"Money, dum-dum!"

"Cash, you mean. Why should there be any more?"

"Oh, don't be obtuse, Susan! You know Uncle Joe had money. I wonder where it could be?"

"Could be anywhere," I snapped, losing patience. "Could be in a box at a bank. Could be in a hole in the ground somewhere. Buy a shovel. Could be in the house. How many millions have you decided there is?"

"In the house." Betty ignored my last barbed dart. "See you tonight, I guess."

She rang off abruptly, leaving me to stare again at the telephone before I hung up my end.

Ten thousand dollars. Dear Uncle Joe. An Eastlake chest. Good God. But how typically Uncle Joe. I supposed I'd have to talk with Mr. Wyndham and acknowledge the bequest. Had the Wyndhams been among Margaret's dinner guests all those years ago? Joe and Margaret had been on social terms with the Wyndhams that far back, I thought. Ask Mr. Wyndham. He'd think I was out of my mind. He wouldn't remember old gossip about antiques.

Now there was a thought. Maybe I didn't need all of Margaret's guests, merely the antique buffs. But how could I separate one batch from the other without knowing all the names? Dammit, I needed the list.

Then my mind skittered away to Betty. Her "see you tonight" reminded me of yet another distraction.

50

Cora Whitney, for her own inscrutable reasons, was extending to Belmont Street what she chose to call a "farewell drink to Old Joe." Not quite a wake. Not clearly a party, since the expected mood was a little too solemn, but requiring getting ready as for a party. I had helped Cora with her party preparations—she gave them two or three times a year— ever since she came to Belmont.

Cora was recently widowed when she moved into the cream-colored house directly across from the Thorntons, although it wasn't the Thorntons' then, for she beat them to Belmont by about six months and watched their moving in with close interest.

At length, persuaded that Pete and Dagmar really were brother and sister, she could turn her attention to the rest of the street, where she saw shops opening all around her. Cora observed, and decided she might as well do likewise.

I felt sorry for Cora Whitney. She came alone and forlorn, choosing Belmont because Margaret Foster was there. The two had been friends from childhood in a friendship that survived because both of them survived and shared memories that became more important with every passing year, until Margaret died in her turn and left Cora alone again.

Cora Whitney's curiosity was legendary up and down Belmont. She watched everything that went on with the same unblinking attention she bestowed on the Thorntons. All of Belmont applauded her decision to turn shopkeeper.

With characteristic vigor Cora, faithfully copying the example of her neighbors, moved her living quarters to her upper floor and readied the street floor for service at retail. This consisted of sweeping out the corners and plopping some boards atop sawhorses. After that Cora hitched herself to a seat on one of her improvised display tables, gazed with wide eyes at the otherwise empty space around her and came to grips with her first problem as a dealer. What was she going to sell?

"I can't seem to get started," Cora lamented one day when she trotted across Belmont to Beckett's to tell me all about it.

I was brushing sealer on a chair, the last of four, when she came. She couldn't sit in any of the other three—they had no seats—but she might rub against them. Hastily, I guided her to a spot where she could sit in safety.

"I've been open for three weeks and not a single customer." Cora turned on me a look wider-eyed than usual. "Think of it—not one. Of course," she added without a smile, "I've got nothing to sell."

"There might be some connection," I said with matching gravity.

Cora Whitney nodded. She sounded woolly-witted now and again, but a fine grasp of essentials never wholly deserted her. "Maybe if I had a name it would help." Another widening of faded brown eyes. "A sign should be a big help, only I can't decide on a name."

I tried to be gentle. "What you call yourself will be more or less linked to what you deal in, Cora. It'd be pretty hard to decide one without knowing the other."

"Yes, dear, I daresay you're right, but I haven't very much money."

I scratched my nose with the handle of my brush for a reflective interval. "Tell you what. Come along with me to a few auctions. See what takes your eye that you can bid in cheap. You never know, there might be something. Poke around among the boxes and see what's there."

Cora Whitney's gratitude was touching. She did her homework, too. The first three trips she didn't bid on a thing, but sat watching events and entering notes on a scratch pad, her eyes growing steadily wider as the sales progressed. I left her to it and didn't pay much attention. I had my own reasons for being there.

The fourth time out Cora timidly raised a hand to bid a quarter. We came back from that excursion with three whiskey boxes, a sizable trunk, and two barrels used by movers for packing dishes. All of them were Cora's. Her total investment was three dollars, one of the barrels having gone high for eighty-five cents.

"The nerve of that man, running me up," she sniffed as we wrestled her trophies into her premises.

"What on earth did you get? These boxes are heavy."

"Paper," Cora panted under her end of the box.

Cora Whitney had found her specialty. She sold one of the boxes without ever unpacking it for three dollars and a half. It was her most serious and just about her only false move.

"There really isn't much money in it, is there?" she asked in a worried tone as she put the three-fifty into her cash box.

"You did it wrong," I told her. "Sure, you bought it by the box, but you should sell it by the piece. Say it's all loose sheets of paper in those boxes—advertising, pictures, valentines, what-have-you. Loose sheets, and you let them go for a nickel or a dime, maybe sometimes a quarter or even a dollar, *per sheet*. Do you have any notion how many sheets of paper can be stacked in a liquor box?"

"Oh," said Cora Whitney, her brown eyes opening very wide. "Ah!"

In five years Cora built her shop from nothing to preeminence in paper and a few things used with paper. Holders, for place cards. Inkwells and old pens. Old sheet music, magazines, magazine covers and tear sheets, photograph albums, valentines, advertising layouts (she did extremely well with a series for Cream of Wheat), mail-order catalogs, movie posters. I wouldn't have believed there was so much to be made from paper goods, if I hadn't seen the results at Cora Whitney's. She never got around to giving herself a business name. As time went on she seemed to feel that the address was sufficient. I daresay the Queen feels the same about Buckingham.

I sometimes had very mixed feelings toward Cora Whitney, for she crowded sharp dealing to the outermost limits

53

of technical honesty. When she told an inquiring customer that the gismo came out of a hundred-year-old trunk (with the implication that the gismo was also a hundred years old), she told the exact truth. Cora kept the trunk out of sight for the express purpose of taking things out of, after she had put them in for a ceremonial five seconds by the watch. Still, that's how a good many dealers play the game.

On the other hand, Cora Whitney after hours had many kindnesses to her credit. She visited the Misses Sanders faithfully every few days, never staying very long but always making certain that the ladies were all right. Let anyone fall ill, and she'd be there to help. More than one of us along Belmont have come back from flu on soups and custards cooked by Cora Whitney.

I enlisted Dagmar to keep an eye on Beckett's and walked across Belmont to Cora's to wash highball glasses and marshal hors d'oeuvres onto plates.

Joe Foster's blank windows gaped at me. Somehow I had to learn who visited that house one evening ten years ago and what had gone on there. A pity that the house itself couldn't tell me. The dead windows stared back dumbly.

I didn't linger in what used to be Cora's living room, but made for the stairs rising along one side of the room. She had added an enormous pile of newspapers to her stock. Yellowed and brittle, they rose from the floor and spilled over onto one of her display tables, where she had already arranged a few to best effect. The one I could see proclaimed in letters two inches high that Lindy had arrived in Paris.

Cora was waiting to envelop my navy blue pantsuit in a capacious apron, and then we got busy.

It was a strange assembly that night. Belmont Street stood or sat in Cora Whitney's living room, ate the food offered and accepted drinks, which they dutifully lifted to Joe Foster, and exchanged uncertain glances, as they wondered what degree of levity was expected of them. There was little of the general circulation and heigh-ho usually found at Cora's get-togethers. Talk started sporadically here and there, continued briefly and trailed off into awkward gaps, as speakers realized their audiences weren't listening.

Only the Thorntons seemed undaunted by atmosphere. Dagmar unaffectedly came to a party. When the party didn't materialize, she just as forthrightly went somewhere else. I wished I had the guts to do the same.

"Yes," said Pete, reading my thought, as he placidly worked his way through a dish of peanuts, "not one of Cora's happier ideas."

Ray and Betty Foster came together and made no effort to mingle. Ray sent a questioning look my way, which I ignored. Turning to my immediate neighbor, I plunged into pointless anecdote.

Cora did her best, but her usual touch with guests had deserted her. Her cheeriest word to me was a ladylike keening about the Foster house—"so dead looking, with no lights at all—" She seemed to realize that it lacked a certain something as a party brightener, for she broke off abruptly, waved a hand in an indecisive gesture, and moved on to the next group grimly clutching highball glasses as if hanging onto lifelines.

Cora kept trying. "We'll all certainly miss Joe Foster, won't we?" and they all said yes, we certainly will, and glumly inspected their glasses.

I gave up on Cora's party and switched my mind to that other party. Were Margaret's dinner guests sorry they went that evening? I tried to visualize that earlier party, imagine who might have been there, but the attempt was a fizzle. All I could see was Cora's unsteady pile of old newspapers. All those ordered columns of fine print. People didn't buy those old newspapers for the same reasons that contemporary readers bought them. The items read with interest now were not necessarily identical with the headlines that sold the papers. Yet the papers were the same, whether an item had

55

to wait a day or a year or a century for its interested reader. Or a decade—Newspapers.

"Why, of course," I said softly, "the morgue!"

"Well, really, Susan," said Cora in an offended tone, "I know it isn't the brightest, but you can hardly expect it to be, can you, in the circumstances?"

"What? Oh—no, Cora, I wasn't talking about your party. It's a lovely party."

Cora's brown eyes widened momentarily at this thumping social lie before she moved on in her relentless hostess round.

The evening's one lively moment was supplied by Betty Foster. She harangued Ray steadily from the spot where they had taken root, her voice pitched just under the general noise level. Then one of those sudden silences fell on the already afflicted company and Betty's voice rang out.

"I don't care what you say. I know Uncle Joe left a lot more money than *that*. It's got to be somewhere—I'll bet it *is* in the house! Everything else is!"

Every eye flicked in her direction, every ear pricked, as the idea of unguarded treasure took hold of everyone present—honest enough, but scavengers all. Conversation rose from all quarters in determined barrages to conceal alluring thought, while I damned my wicked facility for inventing nonsense.

When I went home around nine-thirty, I was glad to see that Uncle Joe's windows were still dark. I'd mention it to Mr. Wyndham. Any unoccupied house in the city was vulnerable these days.

5

MONDAY MORNING FOUND me issuing orders. "And the nest of tables, a hundred dollars. Not a penny less, Dagmar."

"Except if someone offers eighty-five, grab it?"

"No-o-o, not quite. Let him have them with great reluctance."

Dagmar grinned and made a circle in the air with thumb and forefinger.

I grinned back. "You get the idea. Just remember the code and you won't go far wrong." I had spent an hour explaining my code to Dagmar—the inconspicuous sticker recording my break-even point that goes on every piece offered for sale by Beckett's. I pretend not to hear when clients speculate about those purposely cabalistic markings.

I was all crisp assurance as I picked up my purse, checked to be sure it held a ballpoint pen that worked, and added a small notebook.

I had never had occasion to visit our morning newspaper office and didn't know what to expect. I was braced to read page by page. No such thing. Down the hall to the right to a door marked Library. There was an index.

The lad behind the counter looked all of nineteen, combining the acne of late adolescence with an awesome patina of worldly savvy.

"Who?"

"Margaret Foster. Mrs. Joseph N."

"What do you want to know about her?"

"Who she invited to dinner—"

"Can't tell you that, nobody can, 'cept maybe her—"

"She's dead."

"Okay. Nobody." The grand inquisitor paused for effect, then relented enough to add, "Maybe tell you who came."

"That'll do," I said with becoming meekness.

"When?"

I gave him bracketing dates and he said just a minute without so much as a twitch of an eyebrow, and came back in a couple of minutes with a card on which he had jotted a date. Next stop, a kind of side chamber with a microfilm reader.

Three minutes of twiddling controls on the reader while I cranked through the film to the spot I wanted, and I had my list. Margaret had spread a table for only ten guests—a sit-down party, evidently, such as she liked to give. This was *the* party of the season for her, I thought, as I copied familiar names into my notebook: Mr. and Mrs. Daniel P. Limkin; Mr. and Mrs. Lester Rosenstael; Mr. and Mrs. Thomas E. Ellery; Mr. and Mrs. John X. Wyndham; Mr. and Mrs. Eustace R. Starricker.

Dan Limkin, curator of fine arts, had been Hank's good friend, and still counted himself, at least verbally, as friend of Hank Beckett. I could see him without much difficulty.

Likewise, Mr. Wyndham, Joe Foster's lawyer and the lightweight in this company of antiques expertise. Nonetheless, his impressions could be useful, once I jostled him into recalling his impressions. My. Wyndham was also accessible.

Lester Rosenstael was a different story. Museum director—Dan Limkin's boss—Mr. Rosenstael ruled in splendid isolation. Rumor had it that nobody, including God, saw Mr. Rosenstael without an appointment, and while he might unbend for God, provided His credentials were in order, he sure as hell didn't admit anyone else.

And what of Thomas E. Ellery, as full of gossip as any barnyard hen? I knew Tee Ellery, as I knew most of the city's gallery owners, and didn't doubt that I could see him. How could I pick his brain without activating his clucking reflex?

What also of Eustace Starricker? His gallery had been new on the scene ten years ago. What could he have noticed that would be significant now?

"You find what you want?"

"Hm-m? Oh—yes, thank you. You can have it back now."

My watch said eleven-ten when I emerged onto the street. Too late to tackle anyone before noon, so I stood myself an early lunch and sat long over coffee, with my notebook open on the table.

What were the right questions to ask these five men? What, exactly, did I hope to learn from them? When I got to Mr. Wyndham, alert him about the Foster house at the same time. I made a note beside Mr. Wyndham's name.

As I sat musing and sipping extra cups of coffee that I didn't want, I tried to imagine the scene of that long-ago dinner party in a house now dead. Margaret, fragile but animated, preening herself a bit on her coup in luring both the Rosenstaels and the Starrickers to her table—in her reckoning, both the monarch of the art world and her very own discovery. Well, there was no denying that Starricker's fortunes had been enhanced by Margaret Foster's patronage, and no denying that Lester Rosenstael's eminence was more than local.

Bluff, hearty Joe was there, of course, showing off his new toy, his very fine Chippendale highboy. Very fine because his trusted friend, Hank Beckett, said it was very fine.

Had they put the highboy in the dining room? Odd, somehow, that I could see those assorted guests of the evening, but couldn't visualize the first detail of the highboy that brought them together. I had seen Chippendale highboys aplenty, but never the Foster highboy, which made all the difference.

Those dinner guests, though, saw it. Ask them to describe it. That should be a right question. I entered it in my notebook and contemplated it with a frown. I wanted a little more than that.

What did Joe and Margaret say about it beforehand to those five couples, I wondered suddenly. "Come to dinner, see our new highboy certified by Hank Beckett—you know Dr. Beckett, of course. Pity he's on the West Coast now and can't join us." Something like that? Or did they ring in the highboy as a surprise to entertain guests? Well, it did that. Hilarious, to find out Beckett could be so wrong—or so devious. Margaret must have said something in advance. The highboy was her lure, so to speak. I made another entry in my notebook.

What else? Again, I pictured Margaret Foster's house in party dress, guests chit-chatting back and forth. At some point they saw the highboy, and the party mood changed. Very well, what did they see? What did they notice about that piece of furniture to make them think it was all wrong? How soon did they notice it? Surely not right away. Hank would have seen anything obvious.

I saw that I was tracing aimless circles into my notebook, doodled counterpart to the circle of my thought.

"The only way to find out, Susan, is to ask," I scolded under my breath. Closing the notebook with a snap, I restored it to my purse, laid down change for the tip, paid the check, and made for the nearest telephone.

I started with Dan Limkin, easiest to see. He was back from lunch when I called and yes, he would see me. I hung up the phone, then paused and after a little more reflection made two more calls.

Tee Ellery's interest was a cinch to capture. "How about taking me to dinner tonight, Tee?"

"Yes, Susan, of course. Seven-thirty, dear. I'll pick you up."

When I hung up the phone I could all but see his nose twitch with the scent of gossip.

I checked the next number in the book and dialed again.

Eustace Starricker might not be so easy. Not a friend of the family like Dan Limkin, neither did Starricker share Tee's penchant for hearing the promise of another juicy morsel in every utterance. Still, we were on "Stace" and "Susan" terms, and it was the first of the week for Stace as much as for the rest of us. Business ought to be a little slow for him too.

"Stace? Susan Beckett here. Look, Stace, when's the first time I can see you? I want to ask something about a high-boy."

"Oh. Well, how about tomorrow morning, say around ten?"

"If that's the best you can do, okay."

"It's the best I can do. Auction up-county tonight."

So there was. I had planned to go and forgotten all about it.

"Ten o'clock tomorrow, then. I'll bring some doughnuts, Stace, we can have an early coffee break."

Eustace Starricker laughed. "For doughnuts, I'll tell all."

"I'm counting on it," I told him sweetly and went out to hail a cab.

Dan Limkin had aged. Chiefly, he had gained weight that ill became him. Where some carry fifty or sixty extra pounds with aplomb approaching majesty, Dan's extra chins seemed to depress him. In addition, he had lost all his hair except for a two-inch band that circled his head just above his ears, and had developed a trick of fingering the fringe from time to time, as if to reassure himself that it was still there.

But he was as amiably cordial as ever to Hank Beckett's daughter as he ushered me into his office and into a chair, taking his own place behind his desk and courteously pretending not to see that ten years had wrought a few changes in me, too. From a scared seventeen, I had gone to a worried twenty-seven, accustomed to going it alone, tougher on the surface, but still secretly afraid. Where seventeen feared

61

perpetual ambiguity about that highboy, twenty-seven feared proof in the wrong direction.

Dan Limkin and I studied each other silently for a few seconds.

"What can I do for you, Susan?" he said then. "You said, something about a highboy?"

"Yes, Dan, a highboy." I took a deep breath and plunged. "The Foster highboy, Dan, the one Hank appraised."

Dan Limkin winced. His hand strayed upward to his fringe of hair.

"Dan, what really happened that night? You were there."

"Susan," he pleaded, "it was a long time ago. You can't expect me to remember after ten years."

"You remember something," I pressed, "tell me what you do remember. Where was it, in the drawing room?"

Dan shook his head. "No. *We* were in the drawing room—you're right, Susan, parts do come back—until everybody came. The Rosenstaels came last, as I recall."

"Were the doors closed between the rooms?"

"Yes, I'm sure of that."

"So what happened? You were all together having drinks, I suppose, and then—"

"Then dinner was announced. Joe pushed back the doors while Margaret fluttered about their great collecting coup."

"What did she say, Dan, as nearly as you recall?"

"Why, only that they were very proud of finding it and fortunate in being able to call on Hank for his judgment that it was worth what they paid."

"Did Margaret say how much they paid?"

An unhappy nod. "She said eight thousand, boasting a little, you know, about their bargain."

"Dan, you saw it. I never have. What was it like?"

"What do you mean, what was it like? Scroll top, ball-and-claw feet, carved shell in the apron—Chippendale highboy."

"What didn't you like about it?"

"Oh, it wasn't a bad piece, Susan," Dan Limkin said, so

62

quickly that I could guess he had said the same thing to himself many times in ten years. "Not bad at all. For a while it looked very good. The finish was intact—" He meant the original finish. "And I will say," he added reflectively, "I thought the legs were all original, too." They aren't always.

Dan had closed his eyes, as if to visualize better the merits of the Foster highboy. "It wasn't a bad piece, Susan," he said again.

"But not worth eight thousand dollars," I said softly.

Dan Limkin opened his eyes. "No," unhappily, "not eight thousand. Two, maybe. Three, at most. Not eight."

We gazed at each other sadly, both of us struck temporarily dumb.

Dan recovered first, clearing his throat mightily and shifting objects on his desk with ferocious energy. "It was very difficult for all of us."

"Did it ever occur to anyone that maybe Hank Beckett didn't make a mistake after all—"

A startled expression appeared in Dan Limkin's eyes, stopping me in mid-flight.

"We-l-l-l," he said, drawing it out.

"Thanks, Dan. Thanks a lot." So it had all been decided a long time ago. I stood up to go.

"One more question, Dan, before I leave you to your golden memories of friends gone wrong."

"Now, Susan, you're not being fair."

"What's fair got to do with it?" I said from the depths of bitterness.

Dan Limkin shifted his blotter pad a trifle to the left, shifted it back, avoiding my eyes. He stood then, behind his desk, and spoke with unexpected dignity.

"I spent much thought at the time, Susan, trying to find some more—ah—congenial solution to a-a-an unpalatable conundrum. I finally learned to put it out of mind. What was done was done, and I couldn't change any part of it. Now you're saying I jumped to conclusions. No, Susan. What were we supposed to think? Hank never said one word in his own defense. In fact—" Dan stopped.

"In fact, what?" Suddenly my throat felt dry.

Dan squared his shoulders, bracing himself. "In fact, the contrary, maybe. I never told you, Susan."

"What are you saying, Dan?"

"Hank was still in the hospital," Dan Limkin said unwillingly, "and the highboy—it was on his mind. I don't know what he said about it—it was fourth-hand by the time it got to me—and one doesn't ask questions of a man as sick as Hank was—but he must have said something."

"What did you hear, when it got to you?"

"That he'd been wrong—or had done wrong—I don't know which—"

I managed to say, "Hank would have admitted a mistake," before anger surged again to my rescue. "But not that he'd *done* wrong—not that kind of wrong—not a fraud! He wouldn't, Dan. *He didn't.*"

"Then why didn't he speak up?"

"You said it—a man as sick as Hank—"

"I know that—" impatiently—"but Hank got better, for a while. He could have offered *some* explanation—we'd have accepted it—but he never did. Not a word. I didn't jump to any conclusion, Susan, neither I nor others I could name. We felt that one conclusion was forced upon us. Having said that, I'll say more. No one could be happier than I to find out I've been wrong."

"I know you would, Dan."

"Thank you," he said, still very much on his dignity. "You said you had another question."

"Yes. Is Mr. Rosenstael in his office today? Yes or no."

Dan was startled. "Yes," he said before he could recall the word.

According to legend, hapless museum clerks had been fired for betraying Lester Rosenstael's presence on the premises.

64

"If you say I said so, I shall deny it. Categorically," Dan added, lending frail credence to the legend. He was no clerk to be fired out of hand, yet one did not lightly incur Mr. Rosenstael's wrath.

"Thanks, Dan." And this time I smiled faintly over the words, "I'll never tell."

As I crossed his secretary's office to the hall door, I glanced back. Dan Limkin was mopping his brow in fervent swipes with one hand while he reached for the telephone with the other.

Mr. Rosenstael's office was just down the corridor. He might be anywhere, but I was banking that Dan Limkin blurted out the truth. That reach for the phone was the clincher. If I moved fast I might corner Lester Rosenstael before he got away, provided I got past Mrs. Wannamaker, who had come to Mr. Rosenstael's office for her first job interview and was still there.

"Yes? Can I help you?" Mrs. Wannamaker's tone rested nicely on the borderline between indifference and professional warmth.

"I've come to see Mr. Rosenstael. No, I do not have an appointment. But I want to see him."

"Mr. Rosenstael is not in." Mrs. Wannamaker fell back smoothly to a prepared position that she could defend indefinitely.

"I've reason to think he is." I raised my voice, pitching it to carry past the door behind her. "I've got all day. I'll wait."

Mrs. Wannamaker disciplined a faint twitch of uncertainty and repeated her formula. "Mr. Rosenstael is not in."

My voice went up another notch. "I intend to see Mr. Rosenstael. I don't mind a bit creating a scene until I do."

While the perfect secretary meditated her best course, the door behind her flew open.

"Come on in, Susan. I've been expecting you, Dan said you were headed this way."

With all flags set, I sailed into the forbidden sanctum,

seated myself without invitation and waited while Lester Rosenstael shut the door and claimed his place behind the aseptically modern desk.

Mr. Rosenstael cultivated a resemblance to Satan in popular art—black hair, Vandyke beard. Mind over matter. In his youth Lester Rosenstael rowed for Princeton, I think, or maybe Cornell. He still retained the figure of youth, but I nursed an awful suspicion that this, too, depended on art instead of nature. Corset stays, not push-ups at the gym.

Yet for all his theatrics, Lester Rosenstael was no amateur when it came to antiques, belonging to that exalted dozen of which Hank Beckett had been one.

"Now what's all this about?"

"Didn't Dan tell you?"

"Dan didn't have much time." Mr. Rosenstael permitted himself a brief smile that stopped before it reached his eyes.

"Oh." I recited the chronology of the Foster party as Dan Limkin had given it to me. "Does all that square with your memory of what happened?"

He considered. Then, "Substantially, yes."

"All right. What didn't you like about that highboy? What was wrong with it?"

Mr. Rosenstael gave me a reproachful look. "You know better than that, Susan."

I did know better. The expert may be unable to say why he dislikes a piece, while remaining quite certain that he does. It was what Hank meant by listening to the piece. Still, Lester Rosenstael wasn't given to inarticulate broodings.

"There must have been something about it that you noticed."

"Oh, all right. The shell on the apron. It was good. It could have been stronger," Mr. Rosenstael tossed out as one choosing at random. When he went on, Mr. Rosenstael sounded angry. "I respected Hank Beckett in the old days. I'd almost succeeded in forgetting it. Just couldn't leave well enough alone, could you?"

66

"No. It's already been left along too long. Now I'm asking. Was there anything about that party, anything at all, that you noticed, enough to remember it now?"

Mr. Rosenstael closed his eyes and took his time. When he opened them, his gaze was very intent over my head. "Yes," he said across a span of ten years, "there was a— charge in those rooms that evening, Susan. A great—tension, as of—of malice?" His eyes focused on me. "I can't be sure now, but—tension." Mr. Rosenstael nodded once. "That, certainly."

I stared at him. Lester Rosenstael didn't preserve his eminence as museum director by being impervious to nuances.

"From whom?"

"There I can't help you. I don't know. But great tension. It was in the air."

6

PERSONAL VANITY WAS not part of Tee Ellery's makeup. As full of mischief as a cage full of monkeys—there was a more than passing resemblance, too—Tee was not vain. "With a map like mine, who could afford it?"

He substituted vanity about the appearance of women he was seen with. Tee was formerly married to a strikingly lovely strawberry blond. She set an exalted standard for her successors. While Tee didn't expect beauty in face or figure of every luncheon partner or cocktail companion, he did demand that she be beautifully turned out.

He did his own part nobly. Dinner with Tee meant soft lights, real linen, imposing menu and fleet-footed service.

I don't habitually bother much beyond lipstick. So when I glanced out the window to rest my eyes from the rigors of brushing on mascara and caught a flicker of light where none should be, the fact didn't register right away. It did a few minutes later and I looked again.

Belmont Street drowsed under the early streetlights. The only people in view belonged to Belmont. Almost directly across, the younger Miss Sanders stood chatting with Cora on Cora's doorstep. Farther up, beyond the Foster house, an apartment dweller whom I knew only by sight bore a brown paper bag that said groceries.

"Must have been a reflection," I muttered.

Tee Ellery made me wait until the coffee came before he would consent to discuss anything beyond seafood versus lamb and cheesecake for dessert. But over coffee he relented.

69

"Well, dear, what's this about a highboy?" Tee Ellery's eyes danced with mischief.

"Not *a* highboy. The highboy. As you damned well know." My tone would have curdled cream, but Tee only smirked and waited. "What's the word going round now about it, Tee?"

"We-l-l—there's been some talk, since you brought it all up again."

"I'll bet there has."

"I can't vouch for this"—Tee never vouched for a thing; it was how he escaped lynching—"but there are those who are supposed to have thought at the time Dr. Beckett had gone a trifle bananas. They were happy to hang it all on incipient heart attacks—*then*. But now they're not so sure. If you take my meaning."

"Sure. You mean now everyone's decided Hank knew exactly what he was doing."

"You said it," Tee murmured, "not me."

Was that the possible malice Mr. Rosenstael remembered? I knew Tee had never liked Hank much, but what I sensed in Tee wasn't an old grudge against Hank Beckett so much as a more recent one against Hank's daughter. Beckett's, of Belmont had been giving Tee Ellery's shop a good brisk run for its money recently, and he was smarting from the competition. A few good sales at my expense would soothe his sore spots, or, maybe, an appeal to superior expertise.

"Tee. Let's skip all the how-much-did-you-feed-the-chatter and the why-dear-not-a-word. I've got a question, or maybe two, and I think you'd know the answer, and I'm not sure anybody else does. And I'd be grateful for a straight answer, Tee."

When Tee Ellery's face dropped into repose, it was easy to believe that he had just come down out of a tree. Tee looked at me with sad, haunted eyes and said, "What's the question?"

I rearranged the salt and pepper while I arranged words in my mind. "Lester Rosenstael said that he could feel tension in the air when Margaret Foster unveiled her great buy. After ten years, Tee, that was what he remembered most about that misbegotten dinner. So the question—first question—is, were you aware of anything of the sort?"

"Tension," repeated Tee, adding reflectively, "dear Lester, such an unerring choice of word." Tee ruminated awhile longer, pursing and relaxing his lips in a way he has when thinking deeply.

"Well, yes, Susan," he said after he made up his mind. "Tension is a good word." Then he laughed in my face and waited.

"You never really liked Hank very much, did you, Tee?" I spoke my earlier thought aloud.

"I can forgive any man except when he's right."

There was the authentic sound of old resentment. There, Tee gave me a real piece of information. While Hank Beckett had been among those in the first rank, Tee Ellery had been still reaching for that high circle. He was closer now, if not quite there yet.

"Thanks, Tee," I answered the spirit behind the words.

"I didn't dislike Hank." Tee laughed again, his moment of self-revelation behind him. "*My* heart's in the right place. Would I have gone to see him otherwise?"

"Gone to see him? Where?"

"In the hospital. I was in the neighborhood, so stopped in. You mean," said Tee, his eyes mocking, "you never knew?"

"No," soberly, "I never knew. Thanks, Tee, that was decent of you."

"Don't mention it."

"When were you there?"

"Oh, I don't know. Hank had been incarcerated a month or so. I didn't stay long, not over five, ten minutes. Having visitors seemed to upset him, so I left. What else did you want to know?" he wound up abruptly.

71

"About the highboy. What would you have said the Foster highboy was worth?"

"Not one cent over twenty-five hundred," Tee said promptly. He stopped, pursed his lips. "Twenty-five hundred. Absolute top."

"Dan Limkin said two thousand, maybe three."

"Dan's a dear, dear, generous soul."

"Well, you and he aren't too far apart."

"Susan, you wound me. My best friend never accused me of generosity."

"Oh, stop it, Tee. Tell me, what'd you think of the Foster highboy?"

"It was all right."

I tried again. "What didn't you like about it?"

"Mm-m-m—it was a trifle knee-sy. Just a trifle."

I knew what he meant. The eighteenth century cabriole leg was beyond the technical capacity of half the cabinet-makers of the time. Legs were fashioned too short, or the upper curves too bulky, or the feet turned at an angle a trifle wrong, suggesting a top-heavy torso in a half squat, knees turned out, waiting on the command for a deep knee bend. "Down! Up!"

Tee gave me time to assimilate the detail of the legs. Then, being Tee, he couldn't resist a last little half turn of the knife.

"We were told beforehand—at least, Margaret told me, I assume she told the others, too—that we were to see a highboy passed on by the one and only Dr. Henry Beckett. I will say, Susan, that I was—er, surprised—to see that piece instead of something better."

"Try and stop you! How many times have you said it in the past ten years?"

"Well, dear, I did just wonder how he justified his judgment."

So did I. *Hank, how could you!*

We didn't prolong the evening. Tee deposited me on my doorstep with formal thanks for a delightful evening, to which I made ritual response. When I shut the door on him and stepped out of my shoes, it was little past ten o'clock.

Discouragement nipped at my heels and hummed a lull-aby of despair as I paced restlessly about my room. What had I accomplished so far with my flailing about? It was like beating the air with a stick. Everything was just the same as it had been for ten years.

Not quite, discouragement crooned, you made a few people look backward. Yes, and all I did was harden conviction, my interior dialogue continued. What did I learn that I didn't know before? That the Foster highboy wasn't so great? Belmont Street had whispered that for years, loud enough for Joe to hear, and move the bogus treasure out of sight.

You did better than that, I rallied to my own defense. Two people talked about tension. Yes, said discouragement, but so what? Tee's jealousy was what Lester Rosenstael sensed. But what harm could Tee have hoped for that wasn't done for him by circumstance? Tee hadn't lowered the mask for a revealing moment because he still resented Hank Beckett. It was only something remembered from long ago. Tee's malice was more ephemeral, a mosquito buzzing here and biting there.

Two people talked about Hank in the hospital, too. The two halves of recollection came together suddenly. All at once I was positive that the gossip Dan Limkin had heard—things Hank was supposed to have said—had grown out of Tee Ellery's visit. There was no use asking Tee now what he and Hank said to each other. Tee wouldn't remember, or if he did, would filter it all again through his own interpretation, but I knew it just the same. And I thanked him for going to see Hank! I reflected bitterly.

Dan Limkin was fair enough to remember that whatever he heard was garbled by the time it reached him. Not everybody would be so fair, although whatever Hank said was assuredly different from whatever Tee said later on.

Still—it wasn't quite that simple. Tee didn't make things up out of nothing. When Tee repeated, with eloquent pauses and expressive shrugs and sidelong glances, there was always something behind what he said. He distorted, but he didn't invent. I could hear him do it—

"I don't *know*, dear—but he *said*—of course, maybe he only meant—but then, you can just as easily take it to mean—where there's smoke, you know—" Then Tee would laugh, while his eyes remained sad and unbelieving, and go on to the next person with his morsel.

All I could be sure of was that I had started, and could not stop. To abandon my purpose after trumpeting it to the four points of the compass would be to admit defeat. I could scarcely be more explicit if I sent engraved announcements: "Susan Beckett, having looked into certain untoward events, takes this occasion to inform the world that the evidence supports the belief that Dr. Henry Beckett did in fact bilk, mulct, diddle, and otherwise wrongfully use the friend who trusted him, and with the world's judgment, however covertly expressed, Susan Beckett now publicly concurs."

No. Damned if I'd stop. Keep looking. What was it Pete said—keep on going over the ground until a piece of the puzzle was left over. The significant leftover might turn up tomorrow. Or I might think of some better plan. Tomorrow. When I wasn't so tired.

I had forsaken aimless pacing in favor of aimless window gazing, the streetlight sufficient for my immediate uncritical needs. I sat a few minutes longer, elbows propped on the sill, unable to summon energy to go to bed. The street was quiet, most of the houses already dark.

Including Joe Foster's house, I reflected, and was struck by a sense of oddness. With Joe a week buried, why wouldn't it be dark? Why, then, did the thought present itself in just that form? I focused on the house diagonally across the intersection, trying to capture the origin of my mental itch. Then I was on my feet, weariness forgotten as I hastily got

74

back into my shoes, caught up my hampering skirts and ran, down my long staircase, out my front door and across the intersection, heedless alike of noise from my tapping heels or watching eyes. The street was strangely empty, with the unreal feeling of a half-lit stage before any of the actors appear.

But it wasn't empty seconds earlier. I had seen Betty Foster as she passed full under the light in front of the house and mounted the few steps to the Foster front door. In the same instant, from my vantage point at my window, I saw what Betty could not see, a light from the window of Joe Foster's house, upstairs and toward the back.

I had marginally noticed the same misplaced light earlier while dressing to go out. No streetlight shone in front of that window. No car's high beam bounced off that upper pane. The sun had already gone for the night. No, that light looked like what it probably was: a flashlight used with a sparing, cautious hand.

Betty Foster was nowhere in sight as I sprinted across the intersection, but I was sure she had gone straight inside Joe Foster's dead house. She had a key, after all. She could simply walk in. I knew what brought her, too. Once an idea took root in her mind, it wasn't easily dislodged. Betty came pussyfooting to the house, well after dark, to look for the money she believed Joe had stashed somewhere. Betty Foster would never make it onto my list of favorite people, but I couldn't let her head into possible danger unwarned, no matter if she did overtake danger on tiptoe. Someone had been in the house earlier. Someone was there now. For all I knew, Belmont Street might be ransacking the house in platoons— treading on each other's heels in a frenzy of frustration— searching for the money that Betty had said was hidden there. I put on a final burst of speed.

The door gave to my hand, and I slipped inside, where I paused to consider what next in darkness that seemed total. I'm not afraid of an empty house. No one who spends much time alone with old structures and furnishings can expect to remain ignorant of their atmosphere. Many old things assembled in one place set up a whisper of people and objects no longer visible but yet somehow alive and present. I hear the murmurings, but when I'm working alone I rather like the muted voices from the past.

I wasn't alone in Joe Foster's house. Betty was there, and who else? There was an uneasiness in the air. My hand went out to a light switch, and then fell away. If the dense gloom hid them, it also shielded me.

Find Betty, and get us out. She shouldn't be very far ahead of me in the near darkness.

"Betty?" In spite of myself, my normal, low-pitched call came out as a whisper.

No answer.

"Betty! Where are you?" Louder, but still a whisper. Harsh. Anonymous. I very much hoped, anonymous.

Still no answer. Come to think of it, why didn't she show a light? To a decent regard for my own well-being I now added prickings of alarm for hers.

A small diversion was in order.

Joe Foster had ornamented the foyer around the foot of the stairs with half a dozen waist-high pedestals holding statuary that was uniformly ugly, worthless, and heavy. Reaching behind me, I laid hold of the doorknob, swung the door to its widest opening, and slammed, and then tipped the swollen monstrosities to the floor, taking simple pride in the resulting decibels. They got results.

"Good Godalmighty!" Betty's voice was a moan approaching awe, but she retained sufficient presence not to scream.

I thought she was somewhere toward the back of the house and made in that direction, confident that my rear was safe. No one could cross that foyer, ankle deep in shards, without giving away his passage. My own footsteps crunched alarmingly until I reached the hall, inspiring a certain thankfulness that I knew who *I* was. I wouldn't have wanted to listen to someone else make all that noise. The vagrant thought prompted me to slip off my shoes for the second time that night and feel my way very carefully indeed, just in case I was wrong about Betty.

In the dark I overshot, poking first into a sort of morning room next to the kitchen and behind the dining room where she was.

When I muttered, "The hell with it, if I'm dead, I'm dead," and flipped a switch that lit a small lamp, Betty tottered in from the room ahead, whispering, "Thank God, it's you, Susan! Did you hear *that*? Where were you, in the kitchen?"

"No." Unconsciously, I whispered back.

"Oh, the pantry then."

"No. Let's get this straight, Betty, I followed you in."

From ten feet away we must have sounded like a pair of tea kettles hissing at each other.

Betty's eyes widened on me. "You did? Then—" She gulped. Her eyes widened further until a rim of white showed all around the iris. "Then, Susan, who—" she gulped again— "who unlocked the house?"

As if in answer, the stairs creaked. My hand snaked out to kill the revealing light. In the sudden dark we stood frozen, listening to the sound of cautious descent, the crunch-crunch marking progress across the foyer, the quiet opening and closing of Joe Foster's front door.

We should have followed. We should have charged from ambush. What we did was clutch one another in the morning room and try not to breathe. What if he had a gun? Betty and I were willing to settle for ignorant and alive.

With the closing of the front door, Joe Foster's house lost its uneasy feel and became simply an old town house drowsing away its days and nights undisturbed. When at length I ventured to work the light switch again, I saw my thought mirrored on Betty's face.

"Whew!" she said. "I wouldn't want to meet that one!"

"Nor I. That's who unlocked the door. Probably."

"I wonder if he found it." Betty Foster was fast recovering her sangfroid.

"Forget it, Betty. We're getting out, while the getting's good."

"We could take a fast look around—"

"You know better. We're leaving."

Betty's mouth took on a stubborn set. I watched her for a moment, then added, "Look, chum. Whoever left might come back. Think that one over."

She yielded at that and let me set the lock on the door and walk her around to Nineteenth Street and a cab stand there. However, I could see the idea taking root in her fertile little brain. If she had not quite believed herself when she uttered at Cora's farewell party for Joe, if she was still acting out a fantasy when she came to the house after dark, dressed in dark clothing in the best thriller tradition, she had talked herself into believing now. As I waved her off and turned toward home, I knew Betty Foster would return to Belmont for another midnight go at the treasure hoard she believed was there.

She and somebody else. From the safety of my room I glanced across at the Foster house, quiet and dark, and shivered. Somebody wanted something from that house bad enough to go looking for it. Who? Well, whom could I eliminate? Betty, of course, because we had been together. Who else? Ray, surely. He had no need to creep about. He had a key and belonged with the house, as it were. He could come any time, openly, couldn't he? Against that conviction I had to set the chilling realization that the intruder had a key. I wondered what our prowler sought so urgently, and whether he had found it to take away with him.

I didn't believe that money in quantity was hidden in the house, but I knew that any stray cash that Betty turned up was lost forever to Joe Foster's estate, as, for that matter, were the assorted bulging hunks of plaster I had smashed.

78

There was no place in an appraiser's report for "dust and pieces, statuary."

I drifted off to sleep wondering who the appraiser might be. Mr. Wyndham should know.

7

I AWOKE FROM a vivid dream of Joe Foster's house with a line stretching from it the length of Belmont Street, everyone waiting his turn to get in and take something, and the younger Miss Sanders saying in woolly-witted anxiety to whoever stood behind her—I couldn't see the face—"I only came to help Susan. She won't mind, do you think?" A second dream voice replied, "Oh, no, Susan won't mind."

The effort to identify the second speaker woke me. As I came up out of sleep the dream voice merged with the words of a real speaker.

"Oh, no, go ahead. Susan won't mind."

Dagmar on the job, and it was eight-thirty, with me due at Stace's by ten. I showered and dressed in a rush in a sleeveless sheath, green piped with white (we get a few days of high summer heat in April some years and this was beginning as one of them), and was downstairs in twenty minutes.

Dagmar was laying dust with a treated cloth and shifting odd chairs and tables to better display points.

"Hi, Dagmar. Don't work so hard."

"Oh, I'm not working," she said placidly, leaning against a square oak dining table to start it moving. I'd sell it to the Victoriana shop down the street, as soon as I got around to it.

"Who was here? Anybody? I thought I heard voices."

"Peter. He needed just a little bit of stain and so I sent him back to the shop to help himself."

The shop was where I did repairs and refinishing. Because it was large, it also acted as a catch-all for bulky miscellaneous items—a couple of old trunks with personal keep-sakes, a dozen boxes of books, an old washstand in shocking condition with assorted Belmont Street keys in the drawer, my three pieces of decent luggage—and tools, which never seem to get picked up except for the chisels and the hatchet and saws. I keep them together.

"Quite right, Dagmar. Sorry to be in such a rush—"

"Don't you want your messages from yesterday?"

"No. Oh—" I glanced at my watch—"well, yes, I guess I'm not in that big a hurry. Messages?"

"Only one, really, I just said the *s* to make it sound better." Dagmar turned on her ravishing smile. There was no use shaking her, so I waited. From beneath the telephone she produced a scratch sheet and handed it over. Wyndham, it said, and the phone number. I supposed he had the will on his mind.

I called and got his secretary and we jockeyed for time and eventually agreed on twelve-fifteen, and by then it was after nine and Stace Starricker's place was fifty minutes away in all the slow crosstown traffic.

It was one of those mornings. Cora Whitney bustled in, filled with the victory of a coup the day before and evincing every intention to stay and Tell All.

"Cora, honey, I do want to hear about it. In detail. Later, when I can pay proper attention. I'm running late now."

"Why, of course, dear, if you haven't time." The brown eyes widened. There was a shadow of grievance in her tone and a suspicion of quiver about her soft mouth.

"Tell me, Cora," Dagmar coaxed. "I've got lots of time and I want to hear, too."

Cora Whitney brightened at once.

It was a scramble. My cab drew up to the curb just as Stace Starricker unlocked at ten-oh-two. I had remembered the doughnuts and coffee and held the bag aloft for his inspection.

"Look fast and get that door open. Coffee's leaking."

"Hi, Susan, come on back."

Narrow in all his parts, Eustace Starricker had the extreme flaxen coloring that never ages visually and a directness of manner, refreshing in antique shop circles, which brought customers to his gallery in droves in pursuit of bargains. Stace Starricker didn't bargain. He set his price. Take it or leave it. Gallery trippers could ask him any question about anything on the floor. Stace would answer, and stop there. He meant as much, but never more, than he said. Wrong conclusions were the customer's own creation.

However, once he was persuaded of a desire to know for its own sake, Stace's manner changed to a subtle attitude of waiting, when he gave answer, that was a virtual warranty of more remaining to be told. I liked Stace and got along well with him.

In the privacy of his office, Stace munched doughnuts with all the voracity of a death-camp refugee and waited for the first question.

"Stace, when I called yesterday, I said I had a highboy on my mind."

This deserved no answer and received none. Stace Starricker didn't confuse preambles with questions.

"A particular highboy," I added in some exasperation.

"I thought likely it was," he said with noncommittal courtesy, and waited.

Something went *click* in my mind. "I'm not the only one to phone you about it, am I, Stace? Who else? Tee?"

Stace nodded and reached for another doughnut.

"What'd he say?"

"Why, that you were asking around about the Foster highboy, and reminding me of how really shoddy it looked."

I winced, and forged ahead. "Okay, so we know which one. Tell me, Stace—you were at that dinner party—when Margaret invited you, what did she say? Or did it come all stiff and engraved?"

"No. Oh, no. A chatty little phone call."

"Um-hum. You were fairly new in town then. Did she explain why she was asking you? To meet a few people, anything like that?"

"More or less. She said, to view the highboy. The meet the people bit was an afterthought."

"What was your reaction?" I asked out of private curiosity.

Stace took the last bite of his doughnut and spread his hands in a gesture of disclaimer. "I wondered, why me? With all that top brass already lined up, why me?" he said when he could speak.

I could answer that. "When Margaret Foster showed off, she liked to cut a wide swath."

"So I found out in due course." Stace looked at me over the rim of his coffee cup with expressionless eyes.

I repressed a sigh for Margaret Foster's innocent delight in preening that had worked as an instrument of so much woe.

"What did you think when you finally saw the highboy?"

"That Mrs. Foster was an incredibly ignorant woman," Stace said promptly.

"What was it really like, Stace, the highboy? Was it really—"I braced myself—"shoddy?"

Nosing into the bag like a ferret, Stace emerged with the last doughnut and ate his way around the hole before answering. "No," he said, licking his fingers thoughtfully, "No, not shoddy. I wouldn't say that."

"What, then?"

"It was an honest piece of work, Susan. Someone did a lot of work on that piece. If I wanted a single word for it, I'd say—blurred. It looked as if someone tried to copy someone else's model and it didn't quite turn out. No single thing wrong at a glance, but—blurred."

"You must have gone over it."

"No, I never got my hands on it. But I did *look*. You've got to remember, Susan, that I never met your father. I'd heard all about him, of course. I was interested to learn what merits would commend themselves to a Dr. Beckett as worth eight thousand dollars."

"She told you they paid that much?"

"I think she told everybody," Stace said with a small shudder. "She was proud of their bargain. When I finally saw the highboy," he continued on a gathering note of astringency, "I very much wanted to see how he rendered those merits in writing."

I sat bolt upright. "Hank gave a written report?"

"So I was told."

"You didn't see it?"

"So far as I know, Susan, nobody saw it. Which was a pity. Because if ever a piece needed all the authenticating it could get, it was that one."

"Did the others who were there know about Hank's report?"

"That I cannot answer," Stace said severely. "I don't know. Nobody mentioned it."

Certifying second-rate merchandise was bad enough. Doing it in writing was a body blow.

"Dan Limkin said he thought the legs were all original," I offered at length in feeble extenuation. "Did you think that, when you saw them?"

"Yes. Oh, yes. I *thought* one might have been repaired, but yes, they were original."

"Repaired? Are you sure? Which one?"

"Right front," Stace said. "No, I'm not sure. Once I thought I saw a fracture line, but later I couldn't find any. Quite a good job, if it was repaired."

And there Stace Starricker's subtle air of waiting dropped away, and I knew he had no more to tell me.

I caught another cab, then dismissed it after three blocks in favor of a neighborhood bistro. I wasn't due at John Wyndham's office for another forty minutes.

My bolthole, smack in the middle of an area thick with auction houses, was a favorite among antique dealers and knowledgeable shoppers. There they retired following a sale to commiserate or exult or catch up on the news. The place was dark enough to satisfy the most relentless seeker of atmosphere. The coffee was of a uniform, breathtaking vileness, while the wine was believed to cost the management a dollar a barrel. The sandwiches, oddly enough, were quite good. Those who wanted a liquid they could drink ordered beer.

I wavered between coffee and wine—beyond the obligatory sip I didn't intend to drink either one—before settling on coffee as the better buy as a prop signifying occupancy of a booth. Pew rent, as it were. I stirred the viscous brew, wondering idly whether it would evaporate, given time, or merely set up in the cup like concrete.

I refused to credit old whispers of what Hank Beckett said. There had been whispers for ten years. Let somebody else make a case against Hank. I was looking for points to help him. With a flourish of resolution I got out my notebook. My Four Expert Witnesses were as one that eight thousand dollars was too much money for the piece of furniture exhibited to them. Their unanimity made rather too large a showing opposite a "1" on a fresh sheet. From there on it was downhill all the way.

Rosenstael's remark about tension rated a "2," with "corroborated by Tee" under that, sinking my spirits still deeper. Tee Ellery on tension wasn't the ideal reporter, if his own monkey mischief got the better of him. Rosenstael might have sensed only a transient mood in Tee himself, and what could I build out of that? All of Tee Ellery's moods were transient. He displayed the emotional depth of a birdbath.

Stace Starricker's contributions, that Hank gave a written certification and that the right front leg might have been repaired, were the most significant bits I had picked up. I assigned Stace numbers "3" and "4" and gazed at them sadly, contrasting their significance with Hank's journal entry about that same highboy.

I had pored over his final notebook so often that the book fell open of its own accord to the fateful page. I kept returning to the brief entry, as if going back one more time would compel it to say something more or different. But there was only the date and the same few words: "Vetted very fine Ph. C'dale h'boy for J.F." and beneath that, on a line by itself, "Feel so very tired." I still had the pen he had used, an old-style fountain pen with a capacious barrel and a point he especially liked. That last plaintive line standing alone— Hank never wrote in his journal again—made it all too easy to believe that Hank Beckett had been negligent ten years ago because he was even then teetering on the verge of a major heart attack.

"Another cup of coffee, miss?" Another deposit was due on the pew rent.

"Yes, please."

I took another obligatory sip and returned to my notebook.

"I wonder what made him think it was Philadelphia?" I spoke half under my breath, examined the thought, and sat a little straighter.

Not one of my four witnesses had said anything about the Foster highboy's origin. They could recognize Philadelphia cabinetry when they saw it. A certain lush exuberance in the carving, the use of characteristic motifs, a slightly greater impression of width, as compared, say, with a similar piece crafted in Rhode Island—all said Philadelphia. Where a piece was made was an important part of its description and a convenient tag in referring to it. To say that it was "early Newport" or "late Philadelphia" was to say something significant about it.

What did Hank see to make him set down that shorthand designation? I studied my notes again. Possibly, the carving, which was weak? My feeble joy in a clue fizzled out. Limkin

87

and Rosenstael didn't volunteer the weak carving so much as produce it under pressure. For that matter, my Four Expert Witnesses to a man didn't condemn the highboy for specific faults but rather a failure of general excellence. "Not a bad piece"—Dan Limkin. Tee Ellery—"all right." "Blurred," from Stace. Lester Rosenstael, reproachful when asked, "You know better." The kind of piece, in short, about which mistakes could most readily occur. "Feel so very tired."

I shut my notebook with a snap and returned it to my purse.

"That's better. You were looking pretty chopfallen for a minute." Pete Thornton dropped into the seat opposite.

I glanced up, surprised to see him. These days, whenever I saw Pete, I seemed to hear a running commentary in my mind. Hank—murdered. By someone who got away with it. But the police said no.

"How's it going?"

"Not so good, Pete. What brings you here today?"

"Preview. A Duesenberg radiator goes up tomorrow along with a set—a complete set, mind you—of Stutz-Bearcat hubcaps."

"Oh. Well, I'm due at John Wyndham's in about twenty minutes and I'm blessed if I can think of a thing to ask him that I haven't already asked. Besides, if four experts on antiques didn't have anything, what would Wyndham know?"

"Ask something else then. Rattle a different cage. Which reminds me. Have you seen Ray?"

"Since when?"

Pete shrugged. "I don't know. Yesterday, maybe?"

I shook my head.

"Dagmar says he's looking for you. If you see Susan, tell her Ray called this morning right after she left. He left no message and Dagmar wants to know what he wants. Dagmar said she saw him last night hanging around Belmont."

"I didn't see him when I came home."

Another shrug. "She said he was in front of Joe's looking undecided."

Where was Dagmar, that she could see so clearly? In the instant I was back in Joe Foster's morning room, huddling with Betty and listening to footsteps descend the stairs and cross the foyer. Had Ray gone down those stairs? Was it Dagmar's feet that crunched across the foyer? If she hesitated before opening the door, she might have seen Ray outside. But why would Dagmar prowl through the house of the recently dead? Simple curiosity? It hadn't occurred to me to assign gender to those feet on the stairs. They were just footsteps.

Now I wondered. A man could have made those steady sounds of descending feet. In fact, it had to be a man, didn't it, secure in his own strength against whatever lay below? I could not have taken that walk. No woman could. *Except a Dagmar.* The thought slid into place, Dagmar, possessed of the frightening fearlessness of the excessively innocent, like a puppy unafraid of lamp cords. Only, why? All at once I could think of a reason. If she believed that money waited to be found, she might go hunting and never hesitate. Not for herself. For Peter.

"Did she say when all this happened?"

"Eleven o'clock, maybe a quarter to."

Either Ray or Dagmar. The time was about right.

"I gave her hell when she came in for being out without telling me," Pete went on in a moody tone. Out of ripe experience he believed a city street at night was no place for a woman alone, especially Dagmar, whom he regarded as idiotically deficient in street wisdom. Dagmar listened to him in a kindly manner and did as she pleased.

I had always privately sided with her, but I was beginning to see his point. I didn't like the notion of someone watching unseen from a darkened doorway, waiting for an all clear. I had never thought of Belmont as a place for the prudent to go warily with every sense alert, although Belmont Street harbored an abundant supply of shadowy, secret places to hide and wait. It was, in fact, a cul-de-sac where it would be uncommonly easy to be cornered.

"I wonder what Ray wanted from me," I mused, to turn my thought.

"Money," said Pete without hesitation. And when I put up my eyebrows in surprise and disbelief, he said, "Think it over."

I thought it over. Since Ray had always had money, he took for granted that money would always be there in chunks, if he wanted it in chunks. Still, Dagmar said he had asked for me.

"I never knew of Ray trying to get money out of a woman."

"All in the family, he thinks."

"Damned if it is."

"Now, Susan." Pete grinned at me. "He's thinking of Joe's bequest to you."

I shook my head.

"Ray could use the ten K's about now, Susan." Pete sobered. "He has a chance to buy into his firm."

"Yes, I know."

"All right, he's going to have to give his answer before much longer. The chance won't stay open forever."

Still, I found it hard to believe that Ray would try to borrow money from a woman. Lancelot wouldn't. But hurry up and marry the girl, and prop his credit with her cash—ye-s-s. I could see him doing that.

What was easier to believe was that he had reflected on the possibility of money in the house and had decided he might as well have it without waiting for the probate court. I could see in my mind's eye, rather too readily, Ray unobtrusively letting himself in for a look around. He wouldn't like to be interrupted at such a task. All at once I was very sure of that.

I took another sip from the thick cup in front of me. The evil brew in it was cold and bitter.

8

JOHN WYNDHAM WAS a big man with broad features, dark hair flecked with gray, and a wonderfully resonant voice that freighted with hidden significance his every routine remark about the weather. He let it be understood that he had transplanted himself from South Carolina thirty-five years earlier; he had an accent preserved in amber. In fact, I doubted that he had ever set foot in South Carolina, save for eighteen months or so in the Low Country when he was in his teens, for Mr. Wyndham was an army brat born in Nebraska, because that's where the family happened to be. He didn't like Nebraska, whereas he fell in love with the South. So he created himself a Southerner, just like that. It was all a game to him, of course, perfected over years of play. When Mr. Wyndham addressed a lady, I always expected to see a cavalier's plumes trailing in the dust.

Plumes were in short supply when I presented myself to the receptionist.

"I'll ring him that you're here," she said, fingering the plugs on her switchboard with nervous hands.

"Yes, do," I said, and sank, entranced, into the nearest chair.

Mr. Wyndham, irritated, had raised his voice to quarter-deck pitch and was being very firm.

"How should I know? Look in the phone book. Try under A."

Indistinguishable murmur.

"No, I don't care who. Someone."

The receptionist, as enthralled as I, collected herself

with a jerk. I heard the phone ring in his office, which was the first door off the suite's inner corridor and almost directly behind the reception area.

Mr. Wyndham's was a mind that triumphed over petty interruptions.

"For my sins, Miss Ethel, and for old friendship's sake, I'm the executor, and for old friend's sake I'll do it. But he left a house packed to the rafters with the most appalling collection of stuff you ever saw. It all has to have a value set on it before I can file a first accounting. Jim Baird tells me I need an appraiser—"

Jim Baird, I took it, was the in-house specialist on probate.

"—so you find me an appraiser, like a good girl."

I knew what to ask John Wyndham.

"I'm an appraiser," I told him, once I had fielded Mr. Wyndham's fulsome praise, *de rigueur*, with him upon greeting a lady.

"Are you now?" he murmured, handing me gallantly into a chair.

"He was my friend, too. I'll be glad to do it for you."

"Er—for a fee, of course."

"Of course." I explained the schedule of fees. I didn't shave them, either. This was business.

"When can you start? And how long will it take?"

"Start right away. This afternoon. How long?" I shrugged. "Hard to say."

"All right," he said in the tone of "Done!" and spoke into his intercom. "Never mind about that appraiser, Miss Ethel. We've got one." Mr. Wyndham beamed at me. "Takes a big load off my mind, Miss Susan. I don't like things to drag on. Which reminds me. I take it you're here to ask about your bequests under the will."

"Well—since you mention it, I was told Uncle Joe was very generous."

"Very. Now as to the piece of furniture, there's no problem. The money gift, however, I'm afraid will have to

92

wait until the accounts have been cleared through the courts, which does take time." Mr. Wyndham made a steeple of his hands and regarded his fingers in deep sorrow. His tone suggested black crepe for the court's slowness.

He could use the ten K's. Pete Thornton's ready cynicism echoed in my mind irresistibly.

"Have you been asked for money against the estate by the other heirs? By Ray Foster, maybe?"

Mr. Wyndham's eyes never strayed from contemplation of his fingertips. "Preliminary allowances, of course, are sometimes granted, at the court's discretion."

"I—see."

"I daresay," in the same noncommittal tone.

Message completed, I thought. Ray did try to borrow money and got turned down. All at once I didn't want to know whose passing feet I had heard on the stairs.

"Miss Susan," Mr. Wyndham turned the subject with practiced ease, "what is an Eastlake chest? I mean to say, you'd know, can recognize it when you see it?"

"Yes," I said, and laughed at his earnest projection of one seeking information, "yes, I know. It's a chest of drawers. Not a blanket chest."

"Oh. Ah. I wondered. Joe identified it with some—er—particularity." Mr. Wyndham spoke into his intercom. "Miss Ethel, bring in Mr. Foster's will, would you, please?"

Miss Ethel appeared, and withdrew, and Mr. Wyndham turned pages until he found the place.

"Here we are. In Article Five. ' . . . do devise and bequeath'—and so on—'as a keepsake from an old friend, the Eastlake chest which stands nearest the door, on the right-hand side, in my upstairs study—' "

Mr. Wyndham folded the stiff pages and laid them aside. "Is there something special about Eastlake?"

"Not really. It's just a style of furniture once very fashionable," I said through a prickle of tears for the lonely man, old before his time, who thought of a heavy, graceless chest of drawers as a nice keepsake. "I expect it's just as well he told us where to find it."

"Er—yes. '. . . stands nearest the door,' and so on."

"Well, can you name anything in Uncle Joe's house, just offhand, which you've seen only one of?"

"No," said Mr. Wyndham after a pause.

We laughed, dispelling the gathering sentimental mists, and he added, "I suppose he meant to designate the most valuable of several."

"The one 'nearest the door' may be the best of the lot. Or it may just be the piece he liked best, or thought I'd like best."

Mr. Wyndham nodded understanding. "Like the watch he left to me. Old-fashioned pocket watch in a gold case with a snap-open cover over the face. Joe knew it reminded me of a very similar watch that my father carried, and that went to an older brother."

"And how many gold watches did you see in Joe Foster's possession?"

Another pause while Mr. Wyndham counted. "Six. I think."

"There you are. Well, I'll get my chest moved out, and hand over your watch, if you can identify it—"

"Yes. Oh, yes. Any time."

"—and get started this afternoon on an inventory. One other thing, Mr. Wyndham, that you ought to know. Someone was in Uncle Joe's house last night."

Mr. Wyndham came to attention, eyes alert. "What makes you think so?"

"I saw a light. I live kitty-corner across from him—his house—and I saw a light from a window. At first I didn't attach any significance, but later I saw another light."

"Same window?"

"No-o. Different place."

"Hm-m." Mr. Wyndham retired in thought, emerging after an interval to say, "Rent-a-dog! Miss Ethel," to the intercom, "Check around some of those guard dog agencies and line something up for us—"

"Not during the day when I'm working," I broke in.

Mr. Wyndham chuckled and relayed the word. He continued to me, "You'll need a key," and with the help again of Miss Ethel, supplied one duly tagged.

I accepted it without mentioning an identical key, marked with a loop of string and a square of cardboard, lying loose in the washstand drawer in my storeroom.

Appraising the inventory of an estate is a thankless job. The estate tax specter hovers, arousing in the most sanguine a tendency to breathe heavily through the nose. Since the tax, if any, is related directly to the value of the estate, all hands await the appraiser's report. No one is satisfied with the outcome. Dull work, usually, but it goes fast.

It was no tryst with tedium that sent me, humming, straight from John Wyndham's office to Uncle Joe's house, where I let myself in and set the lock behind me. The house stood somnolent in the afternoon sun. Hunks of plaster and dust still littered the hall at the foot of the stairs.

At first I thought to leave it as a homemade DEW line. Then I remembered the dog, due to check in at nightfall. Some of those fragments were sharp enough to cut a dog's feet. I found a broom and swept up, chucked the debris in the trash can, and tested the lock on the back door, too.

Then I went upstairs where the highboy stood—somewhere. I found it in the master bedroom. Standing full in the afternoon light, glowing with the patina of nearly two hundred years, the Foster highboy looked good. *Very fine*, Hank wrote in his journal, and so it was. That finish had not been faked. Then I turned and walked away, and that was hard to do.

I meant to go over it in detail, tomorrow or the day after. In the meantime I wanted to test whether a first impression would endure. After euphoria wears off, elements not consciously noticed sometimes return to mind and dim the luster

95

of first viewing. Then a second look can be taken with an analytical eye. It's a handy technique in vetting doubtful pieces and brings to light a lot that might otherwise go unremarked, even when necessity telescopes the interval to the time required for a cup of coffee and a cigarette.

I had contracted to do a job, so I got at it. There were five rooms, not counting bathrooms, on the second floor, ranged around the stairs. Uncle Joe's bedroom stretched across the rear. Ahead of that were a couple of medium-size rooms and the baths, strung out one behind another, all opening off the long stair hall. At the front the width of the house had been divided into two rooms, the larger being Uncle Joe's study. The smaller had been Margaret's sitting room.

I started in the hall bedroom ahead of Uncle Joe's, assigning dollar values to everything not physically a part of the house—furniture, obviously, but also rugs and curtains and the contents of linen closets. There was a lot in that room, as well as the room next in line, including, incongruously, a wall-hung cabinet (furniture, for my reckoning) containing thirty-seven paperweights and two stuffed birds.

Relief over the highboy made the work go well. From time to time I found myself singing out loud. I'd put the highboy down at an easy eight thousand. How had they arrived at their miserable two thousand? Somebody was mistaken, and it didn't look like Hank Beckett. I lifted another snatch of song.

I was tempted to go back right then and commence examining the highboy, but a glance at my watch dissuaded me. Already near six. Food. All at once I was ravenous.

Look in, instead, on Uncle Joe's study, spot the chest that was mine, all mine, and make a fast guess how long it would take to do that room.

I located the chest in a glance, and in the same encompassing glance spotted that which brought me up short: a house key lying in the middle of the fumed oak table Uncle Joe used as a desk. I advanced upon it as one might stalk a rattlesnake. To the last angle and scallop, the key was a duplicate of the one I had used to enter the house.

With disconcerting ease I could picture someone retreating from my fusillade the night before and leaving the key behind. Cool customer, to escape under the guns with only a forgotten door key to mark a momentary attack of nerves.

As I stood by the table with the key weighing in my hand, I was suddenly too conscious of the empty stillness of the house, too aware of how much alone I was, with no sound not made by me to break the quiet. I wasn't afraid, only a little uneasy. But I'll bet I broke all records for the standing high jump when the doorbell shrilled a summons, followed by a heavy shave-and-a-haircut tattoo from the brass door knocker. When I went downstairs to answer, I hung on to the railing with both hands.

On the step was a small foxy-looking man flanked by a large wolflike dog. At the curb stood a white van with "Acme Guard Dog Service" blazoned on the side in blood-red letters a foot high.

"You Miss Susan Beckett?"

"Yes."

"Meet Bruno."

"Er—yes. Bruno."

The dog lifted a lip with the perfunctory air of one handing over a card.

"Well, are you gonna let us in? I got another dog to deliver yet today."

"Oh. Yes, certainly. Come in."

We conducted Bruno on a tour of the premises. At Foxy's direction I handled numerous objects in every room while Bruno watched. The dog sniffed, and turned his head from time to time in my direction. We made sure every interior door was open for his passage, found a bowl and provided water, all to a running accompaniment from Foxy on the superior quality of the dog's schooling. Bruno was without peer in speed, in strength, in silent approach, in steadfast purpose.

97

"We say Acme and we mean Acme. Nobody gets in this house, and I mean nobody, with Bruno on guard. No-body. Without, of course, you know the cue word to call him off."

"I'm sure. Let me just ask a few questions, Mr.—Um."

Foxy and Bruno fixed their eyes on me, a similar intent alertness in both pairs.

"I take it you bring—er, Bruno, nice dog—in the evening and pick him up the next morning."

"Sure."

"Do you ring the bell every time, or—"

"Oh, I got a key. What if you wasn't here? You'd still want the joint watched."

"Oh, then you open the door and shove him in."

"Sort of." Foxy sounded a trifle defensive. "You see, I got a lot of dogs to deliver. Acme, biggest in the business."

"To be sure. What I want to know is, suppose I'm not out of the house yet when Bruno's shoved in. What, then?"

Foxy was indignant. "Ain't I been telling him you're okay, you belong here?"

He had?

"*He* knows."

He did?

Bruno's tail moved once each way, minimally. Bruno appeared to entertain a host of reservations about my bona fides.

"Maybe you'd better, uh, tell him again."

Foxy sighed. "She's okay, Bruno, okay. Goes with the house. Okay. Go ahead," he urged, "pet him. Say something. Talk to him. Shake hands with him."

I gave Foxy a dubious look.

"Go ahead. He won't hurt you. People got the wrong ideas about guard dogs. Ones trained right, that is. Go ahead."

Uncertainly, I dropped to one knee, bringing the heavy head almost on a level with my own, and extended a hand.

"Bruno? Will you be friends? Shake hands?"

The dog moved. Incredibly swift, he took my wrist within

his huge jaws for a second—his teeth left no mark—then let go and thrust his head up hard under my hand. Finally, he sat, gravely, and offered a paw.

"See? He likes you." Foxy beamed, then sobered. "One thing, though. Okay, if you're already *in*, but I wouldn't go out and then try to come back. Or come in of a morning before we pick him up. Nothing like that. See, he can't get your scent through the door, and a lot could happen before he got it."

I had to know the worst. "Has Bruno ever, uh, killed anyone?"

"Never had to. Folks mostly hold still for him. You all through here, lady? I gotta get going. Be good, Bruno. Watch!"

Foxy unsnapped the leash. Bruno yawned widely and flopped a-sprawl at the foot of the stairs. I pulled the door shut behind us, heard the lock click.

"Now, lemme show you." Foxy rattled the doorknob and was rewarded by a growl. Brief, not too loud, but with a world of menace.

"Good boy, Bruno!" cried Foxy, heartfelt approval in every syllable.

I understood perfectly that folks mostly held still for Bruno. I left Foxy plastering every opening on the three exposed sides of the house with Acme warning placards like so many fluorescent plague notices.

9

I GOT HOME to find Ray Foster holding down the most comfortable wing chair Beckett's had for sale, with Dagmar circling him like a little girl entertaining the vicar until Mommy gets home. I had forgotten Ray Foster all afternoon. I wasn't glad to see him.

"Have you been here long?"

"A few minutes. Dagmar said you haven't been here all day. What kept you so late, sweetheart? Where were you?"

I almost answered his matter-of-fact tone, which took for granted his right to know and my duty to report, but remembered in time to swallow my too-ready accounting. "I've been busy. What do you want, Ray?"

"Not what do I want." His smile was as guileless as any ten-year-old's. "Father McMillan."

Father McMillan was the rector of the old Episcopal parish headquartered a few blocks away, where the Fosters had kept up a nominal membership all their years on Belmont Street. I, too, went to Easter communion at All Saints'. Father McMillan had celebrated his silver anniversary at All Saints' the previous year. Some likened the rector to a saint. Others noticed his finely honed sense of double entry bookkeeping. All were agreed on his energy.

"He wants to see us, as a couple, before he posts the banns. That was his phrase," Ray said, crossing his legs and sinking deeper in the chair, "although I'm not sure they're actually—er—published anymore. He insists, however, on the interview. I told him Friday week would be fine."

"Oh. You did. Just like that."

"Yes, I thought that would work out. Friday week, plus three weeks for the banns—silly outmoded custom, but Father McMillan swore it was still observed. Then we can be married, in a little over a month."

"I see." He had advanced his timetable. *He could use the ten K's.*

Something in my manner caught his attention. "Something wrong? Oh—you're thinking about Dad. Now, honey, there's no need. You know he'd want it—did want it."

"Tell me, Ray." I really wanted to know. "Do you remember anything at all of that little talk we had a few days ago?"

"Oh, well, Susan, I knew you didn't mean any of those things." Ray Foster crossed his legs the other way, a man seeking comfort. "I thought we might as well go ahead with our plans."

"Think again. You're a bad habit, Ray. Like smoking." I spun away from him to the telephone.

While I looked up the number I wanted, Dagmar, who had been following with close attention, suddenly spoke. "I guess I won't marry you either, Ray, thanks just the same." She might have been standing in a trout stream tossing back an undersized fish.

"Huh?"

"I guess I don't want to spend my life after all, taking back dresses after you picked them out. Thanks just the same."

"Atta girl!" I applauded over my shoulder as I worked the dial. "You've got to quit cold turkey. Father McMillan? Susan Beckett here, Father, calling to say you needn't hold Friday week for any Beckett-Foster conferences. Mr. Foster made a—call it a mistake. What? Yes, you could say a mistake in timing. About a lifetime wrong. Sorry to have bothered you, Father."

I hung up on the rector's amused homilies about lovers' spats. Just now I didn't have time for his gentle, misplaced wisdom.

"And now, Ray Foster, on your feet and go home. Go somewhere else."

Ray got up at once. "Certainly, Susan , if you say so." He sounded deeply offended and trying hard to be fair. "You're tired, sweetheart, I'm sure you'll feel different—"

"Stow it. Don't call me, I'll call you."

I didn't raise my voice the whole time, but I spoiled the effect by slamming the door.

Dagmar, however, was not critical. "My! You didn't scream at all. Last time you yelled at him quite a lot. Are you getting anywhere, Susan, on all those things you said you were going to do?"

"I think so. I really think I am."

But after I sent Dagmar home to Peter—nice Pete, who was on my side!—I found that my mood was broken.

Over a meal of refrigerator gleanings eked out with a can of chili, I let my mind return to the Foster highboy and Stace's mention of one repaired leg. I hadn't seen any mend. If it was there, the break was important. Could it be that Stace Starricker actually saw what Hank overlooked? I tried hard to believe that that was possible. Maybe it was, barely.

Canned chili wasn't very good, I decided, dumping the remnants down the disposal.

Malaise wasn't so easily flushed away. Malaise sent me from a half-eaten meal that I no longer wanted to stand before my shelves of books in frustrated search for something soothing to read.

Plucking Hank's last notebook from the shelf, I let it fall open to its accustomed place and read again his final entry. "Vetted very fine Ph. C'dale h'boy for J.F." And on a line below, "Feel so very tired." Was it fatigue that pared that entry to the bare fact of having acted? Possibly. And yet— Hank would have mentioned any repairs, no matter how abbreviated his shorthand jottings. Wouldn't he?

On impulse prodded still by malaise I took down Hank

Beckett's full set of notebook journals and made myself comfortable to read. Hank kept his journals in ordinary school composition books with ruled pages and sewn bindings. He didn't separate volumes by years, but merely wrote in one until he filled its pages and then started another. I asked Hank once when I was about twelve, interrupting him as he wrote, why he didn't use a looseleaf binder.

Hank scratched his nose with the end of his pen while he meditated his answer. "It would be too easy to change, Susan," he said at length. "In this business there's always someone to second-guess you, which is all right, you understand, because it's all a matter of opinion, and opinions differ. People pay for my opinions because they think they're better than anyone else's." Another reflective pause. "The danger comes when you start second-guessing yourself. Think about it for a few minutes," he invited seriously. "Imagine you're keeping these accounts, Susan, as one day you might. You notice what you put down a day or so before, and it isn't quite as clear as you'd like. If the pages are loose, you can rewrite that page, expand a bit what you said earlier. Pretty soon, if you follow that path, you'll be bending your judgment for the flossier phrase. Or you've talked with someone in the meantime and been talked around, a little bit, to that someone's ideas. After awhile, what appears in your book isn't a record of the furniture you actually saw."

Hank scratched his nose again before summing up. "Do it right the first time, the best you can. Call it the way you see it, and then stick to your guns. That's the best way, Susan. The pages sewn in remind me."

When time came for me to start my own journal record, I saw no reason to change Hank's method. I, too, make my entries on ruled pages sewn into a cover. Increasingly, I have understood the importance of a record chronicling not only judgments, but also the process of judging. This was what I saw and handled—this chair, this desk, this mirror; this was what I noticed about it; this was my reaction, and why. It's

104

vital to me, as it was to Hank Beckett before me, to enter my notes in my journal the same day that I go over a piece, and to protect that immediate record of firsthand impressions against tampering later on.

I read late in Hank Beckett's composition book journals, proud record of a professional life that ended in defeat. Some of the entries were several pages long, others very brief, with only a change of date and sometimes a line in between to mark the transition from one to the next.

Excellence and mediocrity were both summed up in a few words. "I saw nothing to recommend and said so," one entry read in its entirety, and I wondered what had offended Hank Beckett's eye so as to elicit such a blanket condemnation. A bed? A bureau of unfortunate dimensions? Whatever it might have been, I knew that Hank, for as long as he lived, would have been able to read that sparse report and remember the piece that aroused his indignation. So would his last comment on quality have been meaningful to him, the only person for whom he wrote. Most often, of course, Hank did more or less catalog merits and defects, for the pieces he was asked to look at had both.

Proportion was of first importance. Did all the parts "look as if they belonged on the same piece of furniture?" Were they designed for use by the ordinary run of human beings? Page after page Hank set down his conclusions, and his reasons for deciding as he did, in characteristic phrases of criticism or approval. "Clumsy legs." "Too-heavy base." "Weak, spindly turnings." "Cumbersome; undistinguished." Or, at the other pole, "Boldly conceived." "Very choice." "Masterfully executed." "Finest proportions." Proportion was his touchstone, as if, when he found perfect proportion, he found all.

I stopped reading to meditate his thesis. Was it possible for a piece to combine, say, superior wood and fine construction with indifferent design? Well—yes, I could recall seeing a few such—lovely, wide boards worked up in designs that were nothing. I could also visualize indifferent lines overlaid with superb carving, for the carvers were journeymen specialists. It wasn't the incised garlands or fans or hairy paws that determined value. A choice piece would be choice were it entirely unadorned, because of its proportions.

But I couldn't turn the picture around. I couldn't imagine a piece of furniture with perfect proportions, and then couple that image with wild grain, blotchy stain, inept carving, mis-shapen brasses, or any of the other ills that afflict old furniture. The craftsman capable of fastidious proportions would not have permitted those other defects to go out of his shop. Defects that got by the artist were the ones he couldn't control—for instance, the quality of glue. Waterproof glues came late to the scene, so that wobbly joints and lifting veneers are legion.

Hank Beckett looked with a critical eye at repairs, and even closer at restorations. The two words were not quite interchangeable. The loose joint reglued, the veneer stuck back in place, upholstery renewed when necessary—those were repairs. The new back for a drawer, new side rail for a bed—replacing, in brief, some part of the furniture that was essential to its functioning—that was restoration. Hank regretted the need, but bowed to the necessity. Beyond that he would not go. The practice of creating old-looking furniture out of stray bits and pieces was anathema.

"It wasn't that I objected to my client's spending her money on it, if that was what she wanted," he wrote. "It was her money to do with as she pleased, and of course some of these made-up pieces are quite pretty in an ordinary way."

My eyes were turning gritty, but still I read on, scanning for comments on repairs. Repairs to legs were sometimes minor, I read. But in the very next entry Hank wrote unequivocally that repairs to front legs were usually major. Repairs to legs with ball-and-claw feet were always major. And a few pages later, "any piece heavily restored can be valued at no more than a fraction of its worth if in mint condition." —✳—

Stace Starricker said the Foster highboy might have been repaired. Stiff from sitting so long, I stumbled to my feet and rummaged in my purse for my notebook. Right front leg. I had written down his answer as he gave it. Since it came from Stace, I would in no way be surprised to find evidence on that leg of *some* work done there, which could account, all by itself, for any low estimate of worth. But not for Hank Beckett's high one.

Wearily I went to bed, to sleep in heavy snatches and dream again in fragments, and wake unable to recall what I dreamed.

10

I woke at seven-thirty to the sound of cheerful, tuneless singing rising from downstairs. Dagmar was already on the job. Reluctantly I levered myself out of bed and made for the shower. Curried and dressed, I didn't want to face the day. The room could stand picking up. I put Hank's journals back on their shelf with much attention to getting them in order. I picked up my own notebook, still open to Stace Starricker's page, and looked about for my purse. There I stopped.

Revolt welled up and spilled over. "I don't believe it, Stace," I said, as if the narrow, flaxen man in person brandished a leg with a ball-and-claw foot.

"I don't believe it," I said again.

Then I sat down abruptly on the edge of the bed, bedazzled with the solution that unrolled in my mind. Of course. Why didn't I think of it last night?

"You were tired, Susan." I could afford the indulgent note.

Turning to a fresh page in my notebook, I spelled it out for myself. No piece of furniture, if heavily restored, could be assessed at more than a fraction of what its worth would be if it were in perfect condition (Hank's journal maxim). The right front leg of the Foster highboy possibly had been repaired (Stace). Such a repair was a major restoration (Hank's journal). The Foster highboy was valued at between two thousand and twenty-five hundred dollars by each of four witnesses. Hank valued the same highboy at eight thousand dollars.

Therefore, if the leg was damaged and repaired *after Hank saw it*, both his assessment and that of the four witnesses would be truthful and correct. Every footnote fell into place. My solution was perfect.

I looked at it again and tried to poke a hole in its smooth texture. The only breach I could think of was time. Had there been time before the dinner party for the leg to have been damaged and repaired? Turning to the first of my notes to check the party date, I counted back on my fingers to the date of Hank's last entry in his journal. Seventeen days, I reckoned, and exulted. Time enough. Close, but enough.

I could picture what had happened. Joe and Margaret got the highboy home, and then, almost immediately, damaged the leg. Broke it off, in trying to move their treasure. Split it, maybe. So they sent it out to be fixed in all innocence that the repair could put back the value. Neat. Complete. All the pieces accounted for.

Now I knew what to look for. Feet, get moving! I hopped up to get my purse and put away my notebook. Pawing through the accumulated loess, I brought to the surface in two or three swipes the Foster house key that I had found the day before. Then, it aroused a vast uneasiness. In my present mood it represented only a small preliminary chore, like polishing the tea kettle before getting down to the serious business of scrubbing the kitchen.

"Dagmar," I said as I rounded the newel at the foot of the stairs, "do you remember—"

Dagmar enjoyed the amenities. "Good morning, Susan! I heard you were up, I've got coffee ready and waiting for you."

Who could resist her unfailing good temper? But while she fed the toaster and fussed over coffee cups, I took my chance to fade back to my workshop for a quick check of the washstand drawer.

One key, marked with a loop of string and a cardboard square, was missing. Someone, having abandoned his own key in a weak moment, had moved with cool efficiency to ob-

110

tain another. Someone who knew about that extra key in the drawer. Not a very exclusive company; it took in most of Belmont. Still . . . I didn't like this extraordinary traffic in house keys.

Over coffee, I tried again with Dagmar. "Who all stopped in here yesterday?"

"Here? Oh, quite a few. For Tuesday, that is."

"Who? Do you remember?"

"Most of them, I guess. Cora—you saw her. And Peter, he came ahead of Cora. Then Miss Sanders came, the older Miss Sanders, she needed more thread, and pretty soon the younger Miss Sanders, looking for her sister. Then let's see—Betty came, on her lunch hour."

"Betty Foster? Here? What did she want?"

"Money, I guess. Do you suppose Joe Foster really did leave money in the house?"

"I doubt it. Was Betty still talking about money?"

"Betty always talks about money," said Dagmar with perfect truth.

I suppressed a smile. "I don't think any money is there."

"Oh, well, I just wondered. She sounded pretty certain the other night when we were all at Cora's."

"Forget it. Was that all?"

"I think so. Oh—Ray came, you saw him."

Dagmar's food for thought accompanied me across Belmont to the Foster house standing bright in the morning sun. She had not included herself—who would expect her to?—yet she had been at Beckett's more than anyone she named. She had injected her question with scarcely a ripple in the current of our conversation. And she knew about that key in the drawer.

I hesitated on the step to check my watch against Acme Guard Dog's notice: Premises Patrolled by Dog, 6 PM – 8 AM. Enter At Your Own Risk. My watch said eight-fifteen, but just to be sure I tapped a summons with the knocker and listened. The answering silence was reassuring.

111

I let myself into the quiet house, set the lock behind me, and hurried upstairs to look for written evidence of the highboy's repair. I expected to find it. Joe Foster kept receipted bills and canceled checks as he kept everything else. While Betty was still living there, she had once complained about all the paper, making much of the delivery of not one, but two, four-drawer sections of files.

"Keeps every drugstore receipt for toothpaste, I swear he does," she fumed, as we watched the cabinets' progress up the stairs.

"Uncle Joe's not that bad, and even if he were, what difference does it make to you?"

"He wants me to file all that crud."

The files were still in the corner of the study where they were set all those years ago, their contents as helter-skelter as the rest of the house. Uncle Joe had years and years of check stubs packed in the top left drawer of his files, with the checks stuffed into the next drawer down. Stubs should be quicker, I thought, for the seventeen-day period that interested me. One checkbook should cover a span as short as that. I could already taste victory.

Finding the book I wanted, I worked backward until I picked up the check he wrote to pay for the highboy, and then riffled forward some three weeks. Nothing. I did it twice to be sure.

Margaret's checkbook was in her sitting room in the ladies' desk there, probably where she put it the last time she used it. The whole room looked as if she might return to it at any time. Margaret wrote just two checks during the critical seventeen days, one to a department store for a dress, and the other to the florist she used most often.

I shifted back to Uncle Joe's study for a go at the files. In the end, I went through every folder in the whole six drawers. I spent the rest of that week and all of the following on those files, in between obligatory bouts with the inventory, and thanked God from my heart that Mr. Wyndham knew so little of how long an appraisal should require. His ideas of timely action had been forged by the awful majesty of the courts.

"How are we doing, Miss Susan?"

"Oh, very well! We're making great progress."

"Fine, fine! No problem, Miss Susan, I just promised to ask."

The heirs were growing impatient, were they? Let 'em wait.

There are places to go where expert and all but undetectable repairs to damaged objects are the specialty of the house. Their services are not cheap. Neither are they advertised. People seek them out and wait their turn. If you are to be accommodated out of order, you can expect to pay extra. I knew of three or four such places of the first rank and would settle for a piece of paper from any one of them. Failing them, I'd accept any of several others, a little less than masterful but still very good. No? I took counsel of my expectations, reflected that work done within the magic seventeen days might have been billed and paid for sometime later, and looked again. No. Not that that was very likely, I reflected further, leaning an elbow on an open file drawer. Those flinty-eyed masters of their calling routinely demanded, and got, payment on delivery.

If no receipt for repairs to the highboy could be found among six drawers of miscellaneous files, then I was prepared to swear that none had been given. That was possible, too, for those characters who were adamant about collecting their due were very often indifferent about the supporting book work.

I went back to the checkbooks, bolstered by the conviction that somewhere there existed a paper record of repairs to that Chippendale highboy. With the stub for eight thousand as my starting point, I riffled once more through Uncle Joe's check records for the following seventeen days—nothing there—and then kept going. Nothing—nothing—nothing. Irritably, I flipped over pages, tossing aside each book as I finished.

Five months ahead in his stubs I finally found a check for five hundred dollars, written to cash. Uncle Joe, as his deposit records made clear, did not habitually write checks for cash. He took out the cash he wanted when he made his deposit.

Five hundred dollars seemed a little low for the quality of work that must have been done. I would have said not a penny less than seven or eight hundred and would not have been surprised at twice that. And where on earth had the work been done, for payment to be accepted so late?

I made a note of the number and scavenged in the second drawer down until I found the check. Stubs were inconclusive. The endorsement could prove my case. Turning over the check, I got another jolt. Joe Foster wrote the check. Joe Foster endorsed it.

Puzzled, I looked ahead a few more stubs in the book and soon found another. To cash, for five hundred dollars, the check endorsed by Uncle Joe. Impelled now by momentum, I found another and still another. Always to cash for the same amount. Soon I noticed another constant, that they were dated on the first and the fifteenth of the month. Those regular checks looked like payments, and I had already gone beyond the seven or eight hundred I thought likely for the highboy.

"I wonder how much it was, really?"

Drawing toward me paper and pen, I went through Joe Foster's check stubs to the last check he wrote before he died, noting down date, check number, amount. He wrote those checks as long as he was able to write anything, although after a couple of years the amount went up to seven-fifty at a crack and later to a thousand dollars.

"Cost-of-living increase," I said, and stopped, momentarily abashed at the direction of my thought.

114

Nonetheless, those regular checks looked unpleasantly like payments on demand. Some of them might have gone as I first supposed, for the highboy's repair. Somehow, I didn't think so. They all went for the same purpose. I'd have taken oath on it.

When I reckoned the total, Uncle Joe Foster, during the last nine-and-a-fraction years of his life, paid out close to two hundred thousand dollars.

11

I COULD NOT immure myself for days unremarked by Belmont Street. Belmont followed my every in and out with the hot-eyed absorption of a ferret closing in on a henhouse.

Betty Foster phoned twice daily. "Have you found it yet?"

Ray was only a little less blunt, after a preliminary telephone harrumph by which he established that he was he and I was I. "I talked to Wyndham again today, Susan, who told me that any—er—currency in the deceased's possession becomes part of the estate—"

"Yes, of course, Ray," I returned sweetly. "I don't have it packed in a briefcase. I haven't bought a ticket to Mexico."

Cora Whitney, her faded brown eyes wide open, was avidly curious and pervasively there. When I had the Eastlake chest moved kitty-corner across the street to Beckett's, she was right there, covered plate in hand to lend credence to her appearance. Lunch, she said.

"Thanks, Cora." I took the dish from her. "But—don't bother." I tried to keep it gentle. "Not again. I can manage."

"Well, really, Susan!" The wide eyes opened further. "I hope I may express a proper neighborly interest and concern." Her eyes slid off to the chest. "Is that the furniture Old Joe left you?"

"Yes, it is."

She nodded, eyes misted, and fell in with the procession as by right. Cora Whitney belonged to a generation whose eyes misted easily. "Such a touching, beautiful thing for Old Joe to do, to remember you so in his will."

The chest was not beautiful. Still, I knew what she meant.

"What will you do with it, Susan?" Cora trotted along beside me, drying her eyes as she went.

"Stick it back in the shop for a while, I guess." It *was* touching—that behemoth.

Cora supervised where it was put, still pursuing her theme, which took a plaintive turn. "I'll confess, Susan, I was a teeny bit disappointed that Joe Foster didn't leave me *some* remembrance—eat your lunch, dear—after all, we were friends for many years."

I started on an excellent cold plate, unable to summon a word to say.

Cora's practical sense rose triumphant through the mists. "I always think," she said, faded brown eyes dreamy, "it's so nice to be remembered in a will." I swallowed ham fast before I could choke on it. "Just a—a token, as you might say. It's very hard, Susan, when you're all·alone."

"Business been slow?"

"Not to say slow, dear, not really *slow*, but—well, it has been better."

When I got home that evening I found Dagmar going through the drawers of the chest while Pete watched with an amused grin.

"Nope. Tough luck, Dagmar. Not a sou."

"Well, I just thought I'd look," she said placidly.

"What would you do with it if you did find a lot of money?"

"Give it to Peter. Most of it," Dagmar added after a moment's reflection. "I'd keep some, for finding it. That would be fair, don't you think?"

Pete thought Uncle Joe Foster's lost money was a joke. "Don't make your finder's fee too big," he warned Dagmar, with a ferocious waggling of eyebrows.

For me, he had a sober word. "Look, toots, if there's any chance at all that there's money in the sock, you take my advice. Call Belmont Street together, read 'em a proclamation, and fire a starting gun. And then stand clear."

I had to concede his point. Betty Foster's shrill obsession

118

had fostered a Klondike mentality the length and breadth of Belmont Street. Found money! Riches for the taking! The mother lode, in spendable form! Everyone knew where to look; it was just a matter of finding a way to get in the house. Hidden money had become a certainty all along Belmont, normally sane and no more venial than any other city street.

If it hadn't been for Bruno, Joe Foster's house would have been invaded in force and carried off, right down to the bare studs and joists, for examination at leisure. Belmont read each and all of the Acme posters, dauntingly unambiguous, with painful attention to commas and shades of meaning. Bruno appeared on schedule twice daily, his movements watched from a respectful distance.

I was known to be there during the day behind locked doors, my arrivals and departures timed to miss Bruno's by about ten minutes. I had many offers of help. I learned to ignore the summons of the door knocker. It signaled only another shy soul with a winning smile and a great yearning to be useful.

Just as quickly there sprang up a way of dropping in at Beckett's of an evening to see how I progressed and whether I needed anything. Any evening found Belmont residents in numbers from three to a dozen parked in my upstairs living room while I passed cheap wine and strong coffee and peanuts and pretzels, and sent someone out for another half gallon, and parried all attempts to find out what I knew. I could not afford too great a brusqueness. I hoped to go on living on Belmont after this midsummer madness dissipated itself.

"Look!" I cried one night, "what do you want me to say?" It was Saturday night, and I had brought home in my purse my schedule of Uncle Joe's payments to cash. "I keep telling you I know of no money. I keep saying anything I find in the house belongs to the estate. What do you expect? That I'll say I know where it is—I know what he did with it—I can account for it? Pick one."

Maybe they heard a ring of truth in my tone, put there by an oppressive awareness of the paper in my purse.

"You have!"

"You do!"

"Where?"

"How much'd you find?"

"Shut up, everybody, and let Susan tell us!"

I flapped a weary hand. "I don't know. There's nothing. I can't help you."

They withdrew marginally in open disbelief. Yet, oddly, while they closed ranks against me, no one seemed offended. My disclaimer struck them as no more than professional reticence. In a way it cleared the air, taking pressure off them as well as me. They figuratively shook themselves awake and looked at each other with new eyes, and what had been a dead-earnest affair of geologists' picks and gold pans became half a game. They stayed later than usual and went home amid cheerful cries of "Mind the dog!"

I shut the door on the last of them, thankful I hadn't been expected to join in the foolery.

I didn't care about Joe Foster's outlays to cash. He could have exchanged his entire credit rating for quarters and skipped them down storm drains for all of me. The plain fact was that I hadn't found one scrap of paper to support what I was sure must have happened. Knowing wasn't good enough. I had to prove it, and I was running out of places to look.

I found my purse and took out the list of payments I had drawn up. That was how I thought of it, payments made to the same place. Actually, however, it occurred to me, the paper in my hand was no such thing. All I had was a long list of check numbers and dates and amounts. The money could have gone in many directions. Early dates weren't too far outside what I was beginning to call, with capitals, the Seventeen Days. Some of that early money could have paid for repairs in installments, to someone with a fondness for cash.

120

Tentatively, I made another list of three names and phone numbers. After a little more thought I added one more. Those four. The absolute front rank in the repair game. I'd call them. If any of them had worked on the leg there was every chance that he would remember. To any of the four, the highboy would have had personality.

Sunday was a good time, so that I reached them all with only two callbacks. It took most of the day and I drew four blanks. I thought I had struck pay dirt at the second name on my list, who ventured cautious agreement.

"Well, I did fix a leg on one like that. Sort of." But then agreement was withdrawn. "No. No, no. I remember now, mine was sooner. Earlier. Oh, maybe six months before you're talking about."

From there it was downhill all the way. I hung up on the last of the four and sat for a time, leaden tired, staring at nothing. Early, facile belief that proof of what happened awaited only someone to pick it up had shriveled to a gummy residue. I was as positive as ever that I knew the outline of events during seventeen critical days ten years back in the almanac. Dammit, what else could it be? But the intervening years had buried proof too deep for me to get at.

There remained only the highboy itself to draw me toward the Foster house. Without enthusiasm I checked my kit for the tools of the trade—rule and lens and calipers and so on—indispensable for detailed examinations. As I crossed Belmont I found myself remembering some of Hank's adages about listening to the piece.

"Let the piece itself speak to you . . . Don't pay too much attention to what the people around it say; they may be lying . . . The piece won't lie, if you attend closely."

Not that the highboy's unsupported word, so to speak, was good enough. I had known from the beginning that for me to go over it and give forth my opinion of its worth meant little. That was why I hadn't *started* with the highboy. I went to it when I did that late Sunday afternoon hoping to see—

121

whatever excellence Hank Beckett saw. For my own satis-
faction I wanted that much.

Belmont Street sunned itself as I crossed the intersection,
enjoying the calm after the Sunday trade. Not many were
afoot, only the Fleatique woman at the head of the street,
busily moving stuff in from the sidewalk, and the dealer in
silver, admiring his latest window display.

I let myself into the house and went at once to Joe Foster's
bedroom. Intent on my thoughts and with eyes only for the
highboy, I got all the way into the room before I realized that
I was not alone.

Then—well, I got run over. There was an impression of
movement, and I had time for a half turn in that direction
and for fragmentary realizations that came too late: someone last night wasn't playing games—that missing key—I
remember falling.

I came back slowly, with a massive headache throbbing in
a steady four-four beat and a feeling of wetness about my
face. Dizzy, I thought I'd just lean against the wall for a moment until my head cleared, and then got my eyes open and
saw it was the floor that I clung to. Bruno stood over me with
a worried look and gave me another moist swipe. It must be
after six o'clock. The dog's tail moved uncertainly as I pushed
him away. I managed to sit up, and then made it to my feet
and lurched into the bathroom for a brief, unpleasant interval that got the world turned right side up again. I swallowed
a couple of aspirins from Uncle Joe's medicine cabinet and
decided I'd live. Discount the headache. My eyes were track-
ing okay, so I would finish, by God, what I was there to do.

I went over that highboy from every angle, while Bruno
watched with grave interest. Every joint. Every inch of wood
inside and out. I took measurements and compared them to
other measurements. I put the carving under the lens and
looked at its depth, its clarity, and where it was and how much
of it and what motifs were used. I spent some time on the
brasses. I found the repair to the leg early on. Very nice it

122

was, too, only by then it didn't make any difference. I wanted to cry, and not solely from my aching head.

I had been guilty of an amateur's mistake. When I told myself, delighting in the sum, that the thing was worth at least eight thousand—well, maybe it was. Then. Not ten years earlier. Quite a lot of trending upward went into that eight thousand.

It was astonishing that anything that could look so good at first encounter could have so much wrong with it. The bottom section contained three drawers instead of the customary two, all of them shallower than usual. Their combined depth made the bottom a little too deep for the top, a flaw of proportion not immediately apparent, and not then unless you *looked*. Once seen, the flawed dimensions made it hard to see anything else. The bonnet was cramped—a trifle. The corner finials were too heavy—slightly—for the carved reeding that was their visual support. The carving was all right in execution and inept in where it was placed. The four legs were a bit knee-sy. Stace Starricker had found the word. Blurred.

Hank was right about one thing. That highboy didn't lie. Inside its fine original finish and quite good hardware, encased within its perfectly okay panels of mahogany, every line of it bespoke the work of a first-rate second-rater. Someone who tried hard and worked long, and who didn't have the eye to bring it off.

12

SICK AT HEART, I finished the inventory and turned it in, and for some weeks afterward tried not to think about the high-boy. Life almost slipped back into its accustomed channel.

There were some changes. When Ray tried to edge back into my life, I threw him out, like discarding a leaky overshoe. I had learned how to get along without Ray. Besides, I couldn't rid myself of the feeling that he was looking over my shoulder, hoping to find Mr. Wyndham waving a check in the background.

By then it was established that Joe Foster's estate consisted of the house and its contents and not much else. A few scattered securities could be sold to cover his money bequest to me. Belmont Street buzzed. Joe Foster had been thought a middling rich man. Where did it go?

I thought I knew. I had seen in his checkbooks some horrendous payments to doctors and hospitals for Margaret. And then there was the two hundred thousand to cash. I continued to think of all those checks as payments. On account.

Beyond that—well, the highboy was a good example. Joe and Margaret paid eight thousand for it. It sold at auction for one thousand forty dollars, including tax. Virtually everything in the house had been bought for too high a price. The Eastlake chest Uncle Joe gave me was as good as anything he owned, and Eastlake isn't front-rank antique. Nor, I suspect, is it likely to be in my lifetime. All of which was Ray's loss.

I had my own problems. I tended shop. I caught up on my

125

clients' burning desires for bannister-back chairs, or gate-leg tables, or whatever relics of the past had aroused their covetous instincts. I went to auctions in pursuit of same. Business as usual. Only, not quite.

When I spent some time at the museum and ran into Dan Limkin in one of the galleries, he understood—I saw it in his eyes—that I was there by design. I understood just as well that his failure to mention Hank Beckett was no oversight. For a good ten minutes we exchanged pleasantries while all the unsaid words hung in the air between us. When we parted, I made a point of sending greetings to Lester Rosenstael and Dan made a point of promising to deliver the message. The whole sorry interlude was symptomatic. The Beckett flag had to be seen fluttering from its masthead.

Even Tee Ellery went out of his way to be tactful, when in the ordinary run Tee couldn't talk to anyone for five minutes without the barbed dart. Tee was a master of the gentle dig, so that its absence was conspicuous. I ran into Tee fairly often at auctions and would see another mot trembling on the verge of utterance. Then the light in his eye would dim and the words remain unspoken.

It was a bad time that took a turn for the worse at the Foster auction, nine weeks after I turned in the inventory to Mr. Wyndham. For reasons not clear when I did it, I bid in the highboy. My peers let me, after a couple of token nods and a faint waggling of an index finger to keep me from bidding too soon against the moose head on the wall. After that early show of life, they stood about in glum silence. Any eye meeting mine slid away quickly, but not before I caught a glimpse of a furtive, dreadful pity.

Tee could stand the pressure no longer. "Sticking pins in yourself, dear?"

"It needs a good home," I answered shortly. God knew I didn't want it. I supposed I could get my money out of it, provided there wandered into Beckett's some moderately well-heeled customer with a taste for second-rate furniture.

Stace Starricker was above tact. "You did the appraisal, didn't you, Susan? Did you ever find the report Hank wrote on the highboy? I've always wondered what he said."

I never answered Stace, but after I had the highboy dumped in the darkest corner Beckett's offered, I thought about it. I had not found Hank's report on the highboy in Uncle Joe Foster's house. What happened to it, if it ever existed? Maybe Stace was taking it for granted. If Joe Foster had been anyone else, I would have said he merely tore up and discarded the report when he learned—I winced as the conclusion slid into place—that it was a worthless piece of paper. But Joe Foster was a saver, a magpie.

Furthermore, he kept the highboy itself. It was odd, with an oddity that I couldn't pin down and that left me feeling as if I had somehow muffed my chances. Yet, what more could I have done? Dammit, I looked. Likely there never was a report. But Stace sounded as if he knew there was. But I had *looked*.

Unless, possibly, someone else looked better? Whoever knocked me flat? The footsteps on the stairs? They were one person, I thought suddenly. One prowler. One secret searcher. Not two. Besides, what would anyone besides me want with an old appraiser's report? And why search by daylight, riskiest time of all? Well, with Acme guard dog notices pulsating on every side of the house, who would risk going in by night? For that matter, who along Belmont, having seen Bruno's coming and going, would take the chance of his being there "after hours," signs or no signs?

I was uncomfortably aware that with every additional logical deduction I made, the list of possible prowlers kept shrinking to exclude everyone but those connected with Belmont Street. Someone living along the street. No—not quite as limited as that. Someone I knew—that much, yes, but—well, Ray fit the requirements. Intimately connected with Belmont, although living away from the street, he surely had a key to the Foster house. He knew, or easily could know, about the extra key in my workroom drawer. He knew about Bruno. Most of all, he was part of the street, so that he own coming and going at any time would excite no comment.

Bruno's furry image raised an ugly question. Would Ray have been willing to leave me in the house, helpless for all he knew, when Bruno arrived on shift? There was a readiness in that quiet slipping away to seize the opportunity, to entertain a chilling hope that Bruno would dispatch the meddler in one of those tragic accidents that everyone regrets. *Bruno* might know that he was my friend, but the rest of Belmont Street did not.

I could build a case against Ray, but I couldn't imagine him as the author of my knock on the head. Still less could I conceive that he cared anything about a pedigree for the highboy. Even assuming that he had somehow run across Hank's report, Ray wouldn't make off with it. Waving it under my nose to underscore the extent of my error—that was more Ray's style. Any other picture was ludicrous.

Every piece of the puzzle that I took up yielded only that same profound dissatisfaction. Either I bruised my nose early on against a dead end, or the clue I followed turned into a glaring irrelevancy.

No shifting of pieces changed the shape of the frame: that Hank Beckett certified the value of a piece later judged by competent other judges to be worth far less. To redraw that picture I had to reshape the pieces, or find others.

Or maybe one other. Over and over during those intervening weeks leading up to the Foster auction, I was tantalized by a feeling of being on the verge of understanding. In such moods I was sure that I needed only one other piece of the puzzle to make all the remainder clear. Sometimes, in moments between sleep and waking, I thought I already had all that I needed, and came full awake while I sorted again through my gleanings. Always, understanding withdrew in the effort of waking to a secret hideaway that I could not reach.

128

And then the dreary conclusion. What difference did it make? Understanding without proof was useless, and I could find no proof. Understanding I had had from the beginning, in a way.

Oh, no, you didn't, a nasty inner voice put in at that point, what you had was faith. Now you've got two halves of a statement that contradict each other: Hank Beckett would not have done that which he did. When the nasty inner voice obtruded, I could expect to lie awake until morning.

During those sleepless nights I could hear Pete, too—"the face and posture of a man who died fighting." Hank—murdered? By someone who got away with it? There was no way to know now.

All in all, during most of that period I thought it a pity that the custom of rending garments had fallen into disfavor. While it lasted, the tatters served notice that he who rent should be given a wide berth. As it was, I could only smile— dammit, smile!—and carry on with my customers. Often and often throughout those dreary, dispirited weeks I blessed their greedy little hearts.

I've marveled many times at the strange variety of goods that will awaken the urge to own. There's nothing so scrofulous that somebody, somewhere, will not covet it. Beckett's does not handle shoddy merchandise, but I do, of course, deal in many items that are not to my personal taste. At such times the point of the question is *why*? Why does so-and-so want this whizbang? I seldom ask. The reason I respect before all others is love.

Very often clients don't recognize their secret cravings until they see the object, when love emerges from the incubator, as it were, full grown. Then is the voice muted, while the hand goes out in a light caress. "I never saw anything so beautiful in my life!" Remains only to set the price.

Mrs. Burton Flaer Montgomery didn't quite fit any of the niches of love. As nearly uninhibited as it's possible to be and remain at large, she jetted her penetrating voice ever thither in search, I suspected, of a cause that would command her attention long enough to use up aching voids of time.

She had lived with antiques and held them in cheerful contempt all her life, until about five years earlier when she made a great discovery. One of a large tribe of young, distant cousins nursed a hopeless passion for a certain piecrust table that stood in Mrs. Montgomery's living room. How Mrs. Montgomery found out I never learned. Perhaps she, too, saw the love light shining. Anyway, she gave the table as a wedding present to her astonished and tearful, overjoyed young friend.

Mrs. Burton Flaer Montgomery had found her calling. In the succeeding five years she managed to give away three mirrors, one firescreen, a bed and bureau, two wing chairs, and another table. With practice, she became quite agile in being somewhere else whenever thanks were in order. In her rendering, she had "found good homes for the poor orphan bastards."

Giving away her furniture piece by piece made replacements necessary, which was how I came to know her, as distinguished from knowing who she was and knowing her furniture from pictures and benefit open houses and such.

Mrs. Montgomery swept in one day, magisterially trumpeting to a bemused friend, "There's always been a table there, Ellie, and you know I'm Old Dog Tray who'll go on walking around that spot 'til kingdom come, and I damn well refuse to look silly! There's going to be another table on that spot to walk around! Besides, the rug's faded and I don't want the unfaded spots to show." The rug was a priceless Bokhara, unfaded spots and all.

She was perfectly aware that the things she gave away were irreplaceable. Wisely, she didn't try. She bought whatever took her eye. Since she pleased solely her own taste, Mrs. Montgomery's twelve spacious high-ceilinged rooms gradually changed in character from Early American to

Eclectic Mix. The stamp of her personality showed undimmed through the transformation.

I guessed her secret the day she appeared in Beckett's and boomed, "What's a good substitute for a breakfront?"

"There isn't any."

"I suppose you're right." Her tone softened. "I've lived with that—that thing for near fifty years."

"Mrs. Montgomery—you *didn't* give away your Sheraton breakfront!"

She sounded defensive. "The child's going to live in a barn! Literally." Mrs. Montgomery launched into a brusque description of the barn.

The newlyweds were embracing one of those pseudo-simple life-style renewals. For a mere hundred fifty thousand, or fifteen years of their lives, they would "restore" a sagging, weatherbeaten barn that the cows were glad to leave, turning it into an aggressively simple country place where they could commune with nature in style and total comfort.

I heard about more than the barn in Mrs. Montgomery's telling. I heard affection for the star-touched youngsters, and self-amusement at the wrench she felt in parting with her furniture, and great loneliness. None of which she said, of course. What she said was, "The old stuff was made to be used. Some of the life goes out of it when it isn't. What if there is a risk the roof will leak on it? Better than breaking its heart! Not that I think Phyllis would let it, you understand. She'd rig a canvas." Mrs. Montgomery delivered these sentiments with a militant air and an eye challenging me to dispute her word.

I remembered suddenly that Mrs. Montgomery was widowed and childless, without anyone whose life was naturally close to hers, and I inwardly saluted her as a gallant lady. Giving away her furniture was her way of coming down on the side of life.

"Well, if you're fool enough to give away your breakfront,

I suppose we'll have to find something equally dingy to take its place. Hide the wall where it stood and save repapering the room."

Mrs. Montgomery beamed, unconscious of the way she revealed her gratitude that her secret was safe. "Knew you'd understand, Susan! That's why I let you charge three prices for everything you sell me!"

"Sure. You don't think I'll let a sucker get away unplucked, do you? Come on back to the shop. I was working up to a coffee break and it should be ready by now."

I gave Mrs. Montgomery virtual run of the premises from that day on, which she was scrupulous not to abuse. Whenever her head poked around the workroom door frame, I could be sure she came alone. Nor did she come too often. Months went by, sometimes, without my hearing from her, and then she'd be back with a new crop of stories about her adventures in Indonesia or rural England, told with gestures and hyperbole, and that glint of amusement at the silly old woman who got herself into such predicaments.

It was therefore not surprising when Mrs. Montgomery appeared at Beckett's after an absence of some weeks.

"Susan, my dear!" she announced her presence in a voice to shatter glass. "Where the hell are you? Brought you something to cheer you up—and you look like you could stand it!" Mrs. Burton Flaer Montgomery believed in direct speech, which she employed with more tact than she was sometimes given credit for.

Her savoir-faire that day proceeded from sure instinct. The Foster auction was two days behind me and I was wallowing in the backwater of depression.

"My God, you look down, child! Want to talk about it?"

"No. Not especially."

"Fair enough. Open your present. If you offer me some coffee, I'll drink it."

I smiled at her over the small package she had handed me. Impossible not to feel lighter of heart in her presence. "It's

132

a deal. Come on back. I'll put the pot on and it can perk while I open this."

Mrs. Montgomery drifted into the workroom ahead of me. I tarried to load the coffeepot and open my gift.

It held a long string of glass beads, each cunningly fashioned in the shape of a flower. Lilies and roses alternated, their colors catching and refracting the light to myriad dancing sparks. Venetian, of course. They make them by the ton, I think, and they're all beautiful. These were superb.

"Mrs. Montgomery! They're exquisite! Gorgeous! I won't say you shouldn't have because I love them!"

She didn't answer.

"Mrs. Montgomery?"

No answer.

I went back to the workroom and found her staring transfixed.

"What is that?"

I followed her gaze. "It's an Eastlake chest. Why?"

"I want it." I recognized the tone. Mrs. Montgomery had fallen in love. "How much?"

"Why—I don't know."

"It is for sale, isn't it?"

"I--suppose so. I haven't thought much about it."

Mrs. Montgomery turned a pair of very shrewd eyes my way. "You'd better tell me about the Eastlake chest, my dear, whatever else is on your mind."

So I told her how it came to be gathering dust in my workroom. "It was sweet of him to think of it," I ran on. "It looks like a pretty good specimen of the period, better than average, for a snap guess—I haven't really looked at it— but—well, it's big, too big for any space I have, and I don't need another chest of drawers, and there are—other associations—I'd just as soon forget, and—"

"And all in all," Mrs. Montgomery capped my rambling, "you're halfway thinking of finding a good home for it."

"That's about it. I guess."

"All right, Susan." Mrs. Montgomery rummaged in her purse and produced her checkbook and a pen. "I'm leaving again the first of next week," she said as she wrote. "Be gone six weeks. That'll give you time to go over the chest and set your price. Meanwhile, here's a binder, so nobody else gets a whack at it. My dear, it'll be perfect for my breakfront wall, and you know I'll be *very kind* to your chest and take the *best* of care of it." She might have been talking about an orphan pup.

Mrs. Montgomery thrust her check into my hand, magisterially overrode my feeble renewals of thanks for the beads—"I heard you, my dear, there's no need to say it all over again, just enjoy them"—and surged out, not waiting for coffee.

Twice within the hour had Mrs. Burton Flaer Montgomery been thanked for acts of flagrant generosity. Empires have toppled for less.

13

MRS. MONTGOMERY'S CHECK and the sense of commitment that accompanied it wakened no zeal in me to face Uncle Joe's Eastlake chest. Although sure of doing right in selling it, in a queer way I didn't much want to. Uncle Joe had left it to me as a keepsake. I felt that I should keep it. Except—where could I keep it? It would be a daily irritating reminder of everything I wanted to forget. Sell it. Except—it had been left to me. Special, from Uncle Joe. While I wavered, another week slipped by.

Toward the end of that week I did sell the highboy. After a few days of sidling past its dark corner with averted eyes, I rigged a spotlight in a clamp-on holder as a counterirritant that turned out to be a merchandising triumph. A sweet-faced, fuzzy-minded little woman wandered in, took one look at my jerry-built lighting arrangement and read it as all the evidence she needed of the highboy's surpassing merit. It was under the light, wasn't it? The third, disastrous drawer in the base was exactly what she wanted. She had seen a lot of highboys, but all the others had only two drawers in the base, which meant this one was extremely rare. Didn't it? I sighed and said yes, it was very rare. Well, then!

I sold it to her for thirty-five hundred dollars. She took it away, crooning over the patina. The little woman was happy with her highboy. For my part, Beckett's felt better without its presence hovering like a vulture over the scattered carcasses of dead hopes.

Mrs. Montgomery would be at least as happy with the Eastlake chest. Set a price and let her have it. The amount didn't matter. If I guessed low—well, the chest hadn't cost me anything. If I guessed high, Mrs. Montgomery could afford it. At random I said two hundred dollars, upped it to three hundred a week later, and the day after that dropped it to a hundred and fifty, before facing up at last to the dismal fact that I couldn't price the chest by any such method. Mrs. Montgomery deserved better treatment from Beckett's. So, for that matter, did Susan Beckett.

For all the years of Beckett's existence, it had been known as a shop where prices were high but fair. Beckett's charged. Beckett's gave value. Mrs. Montgomery depended on that when she left her check attached to an open-ended offer to pay whatever price I set. However distasteful the task, I had to go over the chest. I couldn't depart from the drilled-in habit of a lifetime without being the loser.

Eastlake doesn't have to be ugly, and in all fairness Mrs. Montgomery's chest wasn't, quite. It was just an oak bureau with a plain marble top, incised lines ornamenting the front of the frame, and drawers with inset panels of gouged carving in a geometric design. I happen not to care much for marble tops and machine carving of geometrics. However, the construction was of solid wood, not veneer, and the joints were sound. All in all, in its day the last word in high fashion. It looked like it might originally have been part of a set. My first guess of a couple of hundred dollars wasn't bad. Two-fifty, maybe.

I don't know what prompted me that night to take out the drawers one more time. They had been in and out a dozen times already while I checked joints and backs, hardware and guides. What more was there to see?

I took out the drawers and lined them up and went over them again. Even then I nearly missed the significance of the middle drawer's bottom, because it's impossible to look simultaneously at both sides of a piece of wood. As it was, I looked inside all three drawers at all three bottoms and compared them, one with the others, turned them all over and did the same thing. Still, I had to turn that middle drawer back and forth several times to be sure of what I saw.

Then I was sure and my heart speeded up. I was suddenly conscious of being alone there in my quiet workroom, and yet of not feeling alone, so that I found myself glancing nervously into corners. With an effort I collected my attention again on the drawer.

The bottom was of wood, nothing esoteric. Inside the drawer the grain of the bottom ran parallel with the sides, as it should. With the drawer upside down, there was no way I could turn it that the bottom grain wasn't slightly askew, on the bias. Straight with itself, but not with the outline of the drawer.

I had found a false bottom, not inside the true bottom as usual, but added outside, beneath the original bottom. My hands were shaking when I put down the drawer, bottom side up, and sat back on my heels to consider how to open it without scarring the drawer. Nothing obvious leaped to the eye, no panel to slide, no string to pull, no finger hole, no superfluous brads. I got a glass and went around the perimeter, but there were no telltale smears of glue to be seen. Yet it almost had to be glue or some kind of cement around all the edges, like sealing an envelope.

Maybe it was never intended to be opened more than once. Like an envelope. My heart thumped loud in my ears.

I fetched a straight edge and a knife and calculated the distance. An inch should be ample. I scribed a line along one side and the two ends, and then eased the blade under the edges I had freed and folded back a sheet of the thinnest possible veneer.

The papers lay flat. Taped in place to keep them from slipping when the cover was put over them were a single sheet and a sheaf of five pages, closely written on thinnest onionskin. I sucked in a deep breath and let it out in a long sigh. They were a carbon copy of a receipt from Margaret Foster to one Abby Granger for eight thousand dollars for

137

one Chippendale highboy and of Dr. Henry Beckett's report certifying its authenticity, and a letter from Joe Foster—to me.

I slit the tape and sat for a long time with the paper in my hands. The receipt was dated only eight days later than Hank's journal entry about that same highboy. Sometime during that eight days he issued his certificate confirming what he had seen. And then Margaret sold the highboy. I was perfectly sure that it was Hank's report, as much as the piece of furniture, that she sold. Joe Foster had been out of town about that time, so Margaret had had a free hand.

She had been busy, had Margaret, not only with the sale of one highboy, but also with finding and setting another in its place. Why had she bothered? Selling a piece of furniture was no crime. Unless—the suggestion slid into place—unless she needed money that she couldn't depend on Joe to give her. Dimly, I tried to follow her reasoning: Sell the highboy and raise the money—but Joe might not approve—so put another like it in its place—he'd never notice—no one would ever know.

And what of the consequences to Hank Beckett? A little detail like that, I reflected bitterly, wouldn't have entered her head. Driven by need, Margaret would lie and go on lying, serene in the conviction that it made no difference. She had had a lifetime of practice. She had made a career of selling herself that anything she wanted to be true, was true.

What need could have been so obsessive to spoiled, sheltered Margaret Foster to drive her to such an extreme? I took up the sheets of onionskin. Maybe they would tell me.

My dear Susan, the top sheet began, *If you have found this letter and the other paper I have put with it, try to understand how I could not, my dear—could not—hand all this to you while I lived. And it is an old man's hope that you will remember, as you read, all the ways I have tried to make up for it.*

I won't quote all of Uncle Joe's letter. He wrote as an old

man, rambling a bit now and then, and parts of it were too personal to repeat.

Joe Foster had been away from home long enough for Margaret's purpose. He returned barely in time for the dinner party, and saw at a glance that the highboy was not the same. *"I'm an ignoramus I know, never pretended anything else, I've just had fun poking around old stuff, but I did know that much. I didn't care, if Margaret had found one she liked better."*

But then Margaret Foster palmed off the substitute in front of their guests as the one vetted by Hank. *What could I do?* Joe Foster wrote pathetically, *A man can't call his wife a liar in public.* No wonder Mr. Rosenstael had felt tension in the air!

Hank came home from the West Coast to find the galleries all abuzz with the story. He went at once to his old friends to have the record set straight. Margaret Foster, half hysterical but stubborn, stuck to her guns. "You certified a highboy for us and this is it! Things you certify are important, not everyone can have them." Margaret meant to have it both ways, the prestige that she thought would rub off from the highboy onto her, and the eight thousand dollars to boot. Joe Foster sided with his wife. *Margaret wasn't well, and so while she was out of the room I told Hank I wouldn't risk her health on a public hashing over of what was at most a difference of opinion, that my first duty was to her.*

In other words, Hank Beckett could wait his turn. *I saw his face change and knew I had lost a friend.*

Well, what did you expect, Joe Foster?

For the first time I understood the terrible position Hank was in. He knew what it meant. Hank tried to counteract the lie—Joe's letter made that clear. Hank talked to Tee Ellery. I had guessed right about that. What did he say, that it was "not the same highboy?" And Tee—did he listen with bright skepticism all over his sad, monkey features and then go away to spread the news, "Hank Beckett said the Foster highboy didn't look as good later on, he was wrong"?

Weak, only provisionally alive, Hank came home from the hospital thinking all his world was ready to disbelieve. So he wrote it all down for me, Joe's letter told me—for Susan, whom he could depend on to help—a description of the piece he had seen, the shop where he saw it, the dealer's name, so that the transaction and the piece itself could be traced, so that there would be some paper record in his behalf. Why didn't he just tell me all about it? Perhaps it was the obsession of a sick man.

I wondered how much it had cost Hank in effort to write that letter. He must have worked on it a few minutes at a time, getting out of bed against orders for paper and an envelope. He finished it that Sunday morning when he seemed well enough to be left alone for a half hour.

He had it in an envelope marked "Susan," ready to his hand as he lay in bed. And dropped into the easy sleep of sickness. That was how Joe Foster found him. *I'd been watching for a chance to see Hank alone, so as to talk to him and make him understand.* Joe saw me go out and he came across Belmont almost immediately. When he found Hank asleep with the envelope beside him, Joe Foster took that letter and read it. Later he destroyed it.

He did more than that. Hank woke up to find Joe standing by the bed with the letter in his hand.

The writing changed at that point. *I couldn't permit him to raise an alarm,* Joe Foster wrote in tiny, cramped, pinched letters set down with a compulsive force that drove the pen point through the thin sheet. *You can see how I couldn't allow that, can't you, Susan?* Even in the privacy of a letter that he knew would go unread while he lived, a letter that might never be found, Joe Foster could not face what he had done. The next couple of lines were a succession of fragments, with words crossed out and then rewritten in that same minute hand.

140

Joe replaced the pillow when he was through with it, lifting the horrible blue head to do it, and then could not bring himself to touch his victim again. He meant to compose the body and straighten the covers to create the illusion of death coming to a man asleep. But Joe Foster was through.

He snatched the letter he had killed to possess and took it away. Walking decorously home through the early Sunday fog, he read it again at his leisure. He hadn't been away from home ten minutes.

It was all here. The force that drove Joe Foster wouldn't let him stop until it was all down on paper.

Abruptly I went upstairs to the bookcase containing Hank's journals, took down the last of them, and let it fall open to the final entry. "Vetted very fine Ph. C'dale h'boy for J.F." and beneath that on a line by itself, "Feel so very tired." I was not reading one entry, but two. Hank wrote those last four words upon returning home from his disastrous interview with Joe. Late that same night he was stricken by his first heart attack.

The remainder of Joe's letter was a curious rambling mixture, at once apologetic and defensive. But the writing was stronger now, with the worst behind him. Apparently, he had entertained a clumsy notion of coming forward after Margaret's death with some further tale exonerating Hank. I guess it wasn't very clear to Joe how he might do it. Anyway, he never tried, because at any cost he had to avoid calling attention to Hank Beckett's death. He had been lucky once. He could not risk that kind of luck twice. In a curious way, it left Joe Foster with no place to hide.

But he tried. Right up to the end Joe Foster tried to squirm out. He hid the letter in which, once, he set down truth grown too heavy for him to carry about untold. For the rest, *I hope you may never find this, my dear Susan. I have loved you very much, and your father before you*—yes; in an odd way I believed that, both halves; Joe had loved Hank—*and I hope you may get beyond vindication.* Curious expression, yet I understood what he tried to say.

The final paragraph was an awkward attempt to embroider his dream. As it all started with Ray, so Joe Foster hoped it would end with Ray. *His mother was determined. "I'm not going to have my son in Vietnam!"* Of course. Ray would have been as safe from the draft in college at home as abroad, but Margaret was making doubly sure. Perhaps she was right at that, because when he did come home, his deferment at an end, and was called by his draft board, he was turned down and sent home—aftermath of a shoulder separation incurred while skiing. Ray learned to ski in Switzerland. I finished Joe's letter. *I hope you will some day discover the strength of a mother's love.* Sure. If Ray and I were married, the old crime would dissolve in a romantic haze surrounding the children, as if none of it ever happened.

"Sorry, Joe." Not Uncle Joe. Not again.

Unexpectedly, I found myself crying, partly from enormous pride in Hank, but partly too for the man who had been Uncle Joe, hiding evil behind so much bluff, and real, kindliness.

I didn't weep very long, and I didn't let tears stop me, nor any sloppy sentiments about letting him off free because he had already paid enough. He touched on that with some particularity. Just the same, from the first lie to the ultimate outrage, he knew what he was doing and did it willingly. Hank's mistaken judgment, his clouded perception due to approaching illness, was Joe's invention. He put the story about deliberately, seizing Hank's very real sickness as a peg to hang it on. At one stroke Joe removed the last doubt concerning Hank's guilt. And at the end he killed his friend, the man he had branded while he lived, while it could hurt.

They were all dead now, but Hank's name could be cleared. That much was owed to Hank. But beyond that? Why tell more than was necessary, when telling could only embarrass the living? Why tell Ray any more than he had to know?

142

On one point I had no doubt what to do. Joe Foster's crime tainted everything he did. All those years of helping Susan— how much was prompted by desire to smooth the way for an old friend's daughter and how much by an impulse to keep her indebted and therefore keep her quiet? The cash legacy became unpleasantly like a bribe. I didn't want Joe Foster's cash.

14

I TOLD PETE first. "I've won, Pete! I found it!"

"Atta girl!" His thin dark features lit up with pleasure.

"And Hank *was* murdered. I thought I'd get a few people together and tell what has to be told."

"Tell all."

"Maybe not all, Pete, but enough to clear Hank's name. I thought, tell his colleagues, his—his peers, however many I can get together."

Pete Thornton cocked an eyebrow at the sadness I couldn't keep out of my tone, but all he said was, "When? Do you want me to come?"

"Would you, Pete? Moral support. You were on my side all along. Thursday, about eight. Get in ahead of everybody's weekend plans, I hope."

John Wyndham was easy: hints of a revelation affecting the estate brought him on the run.

Call to Dan Limkin: "You were wrong, Dan—you and Mr. Rosenstael and Tee and Stace—all wrong. So was I wrong. But Hank wasn't, and I can prove it."

"You can! Susan, I'm glad!" Dan Limkin, bless him, *sounded* glad. "Tell me all about it."

"Thursday night about eight o'clock, at my place. Can you make it?"

"I think so." The sound of Dan turning pages on his calendar came over the wire. "Yes. Susan, this *is* good news. I'll tell Lester Rosenstael, shall I?"

"Please do."

Stace couldn't make it. Tee could.

145

I told Ray a quarter to eight, and said only that I had something to tell him. Dependably, he jumped to the wrong conclusion. Thursday I set him straight, while there was only Mr. Wyndham to hear. I had asked him to come early, too.

"No, Ray, I'm not setting the date. Not now or ever." My tone brought John Wyndham's head around.

Ray took more telling. "But you said—"

"I had something to tell you. I do have. I won't accept your father's cash legacy to me, Ray. I suppose you'll get it as next of kin."

Mr. Wyndham emitted a low moan. "Susan, you can't do that, you'll tie things up for months."

"You and Ray can worry about that."

Two pairs of male eyes consulted each other and turned toward me.

I told them what I had found. I showed them the receipt. I didn't dwell on details, but I didn't mince words either. John Wyndham said, "Oh. Ah!" when I told what Joe had to say about Hank's visit when he sought redress—"It was Hank's professional life, you see"—but Ray Foster said nothing at all until I finished.

Then, in the voice of one trying hard to understand, "It's past, it all happened a long time ago. What has any of that to do with us? I love you, Susan. That's what matters."

I stared at him for a long, long time. "Tell me something, Ray," I managed at last, "didn't you ever wonder where the money came from that financed your two years in Europe?"

Ray Foster considered. "No," he said, "I didn't care about that. Europe seemed like a good idea and the money was there."

As it had been, all his life. Anything he wanted. And I had worried about embarrassing that—that overgrown baby. As well try to embarrass an infant screaming for its bottle.

Laughter welled up and spilled over. Helplessly I leaned against the nearest wall and laughed and laughed.

"Hi, what's the joke?" The door of Beckett's swung open for Pete Thornton.

"Ray!" I gasped when I could speak. "He's the j-j-joke!" I went off in another peal.

"Oh, really." Pete turned a measuring eye on Ray Foster, looked back at me, and then he, too, started to laugh. We clung to each other and whooped.

Ray's face slowly changed to a dull mottled red.

"Cheer up," I told him heartlessly between gasps, "you'll get the money without having to marry it."

Pete Thornton stopped laughing and held me away from him. "You're not an heiress?"

"Not that money."

"That's nice," Pete said in a tone of vast contentment. "Not that money. No fond backward glances?"

"Not a one."

"Oh, that's very nice."

Then and there, under Mr. Wyndham's benignly interested gaze and Ray Foster's resentful eyes, Pete Thornton kissed me. No brotherly peck, this. Pete meant it. I snuggled into his arms where I belonged and kissed him back.

"Susan, Susan, I thought I could stop loving you, if I starved love long enough—"

"Yes, Pete, yes, tell me some more!"

"Well!" Ray Foster angrily shifted his weight from one foot to the other. "I might as well leave. I know when I'm not wanted."

"He knows when he isn't wanted," Pete explained with all the solemnity of a hanging judge. It set us off again.

"Oh, stick around, Ray," I managed between crows, "you haven't heard it all yet. It gets better."

By then it was a few minutes past eight. Dan arrived with Mr. Rosenstael and I thought everybody was on hand who was coming, when suddenly people started appearing in droves. Betty Foster; Tee Ellery; Cora Whitney with the Misses Sanders; Dagmar and the Fleatique woman, closely followed by Victoriana and antique silver, followed by copper and brass deep in conversation with Today's Treasure (new to the street; trendy memorabilia). Three-fourths of Belmont Street showed up, turning my intended small, homemade press conference into a mob scene. Ray Foster shuffled his feet uncertainly, but hung around with the others.

"I told Cora," Dagmar whispered, as I stifled the last of my giggles and shooed them all upstairs. "She helped me notify everybody."

Eighteen people jammed themselves into my living room. I knew that some of them would be impervious to anything I said—the Misses Sanders, for instance, the hope of an hour's entertainment to relieve tedium shining identically behind their spectacles, or Betty, or Cora Whitney, or even, in his own way, Tee Ellery. Tee could always make a good story out of carefully selected portions of the truth.

But Pete Thornton would listen. John Wyndham knew next to nothing about antiques, but a great deal about evidence. Dan Limkin and Lester Rosenstael were both intimate with antiques, and both of them, once upon a time, as intimate with Hank Beckett as their natures had permitted. A curious intentness vibrated from Lester Rosenstael. Mr. Rosenstael was not often wrong. Clearly, he found the sensation uncomfortable. I gave him credit, though, for never ducking a duty to admit his own error.

I got their attention and launched into controlled exposition. The facts were there ("the highboy which you saw was not the same piece of furniture"), but clothed as decently as I could contrive ("one of those misunderstandings that happen sometimes").

The Misses Sanders nodded and smiled, not understanding but enjoying the warmth of human contact.

Dan Limkin, angry, shaken to the depths, understood only too well.

148

So did Mr. Rosenstael. Mr. Rosenstael refused to buy it. "We were told categorically that it was the same piece. You were there, Ellery, what's your recollection? Who said so?"

"Er—Mrs. Foster, as I remember," said Tee, with a flickering glance toward Ray.

"As I remember also." Mr. Rosenstael soared above prudence. "She must have known the difference."

"She didn't think it made any difference," I soothed. "As I said, a misunderstanding."

"Possibly." Mr. Rosenstael was unappeased. "But why didn't Mr. Foster—"

"He regretted not doing so at once," I said. That was the doubt I had resolved to give Joe Foster the benefit of. "I think he regretted it. Let's just put it all down to a mistake in judgment."

"Say!" Betty Foster emerged from deep thought. "Where'd you say you found that bill of sale, that receipt?"

"In the chest he left me. When I had occasion to look at it."

Betty was no fool, for all her fixation on one idea. "Oh," she said, "you mean, hid."

I suppressed a sigh. "In a manner of speaking."

"Well! Maybe he hid the rest of his money there, too!"

Half the room were on their feet in the instant. Someone killed the light with a vicious little *snick!* and then we heard footsteps running away.

All eighteen of us pounded after. Swept up in tallyho, no one paid any attention to lights or objects in the way, or to each other for that matter. Two footstools and a magazine rack ceased to exist as that crowd surged through my showroom, while the two Misses Sanders, who didn't want to miss a thing, were very quickly walking wounded, but stayers for the course. I was as ruthless in pursuit as any, and because I knew the ground I reached my workroom a breath ahead of the pack.

"It's no use! I already have the paper you want!"

The room wasn't inky dark. It had windows, dirty to be sure, but admitting feeble rays from the street. In the gloom I flung myself aside and down, out of the path of the murderous rush that went ahead of its own momentum until it stopped with a thud against the wall.

Falling was a mistake—I knew it. Already the figure was turning. *I couldn't dodge twice. I knew it.*

The next instant the light flared into sudden brightness and Pete Thornton lunged over me to seize the upflung arm and twist a hatchet from a frenzied hand.

The light froze them all like so many living statues—Dagmar, with her hand still on the switch—Ray Foster and Betty, reaching for the chest in a dead heat—the others crowding and craning to see—all but Pete and his captive.

"Lend a hand, someone!" he panted.

Cora Whitney was raving. John Wyndham and Tee closed in on either side and forced her down to a chair, where she screamed hatred and defiance, all her sweet vacuity gone. Not a trace remained of the fluttery great-aunt gently feeding on the doings of Belmont Street. This hot-eyed stranger with the contorted features ravened for blood.

"You!" she spat at me at one point, a line of froth appearing at the corners of her mouth, "why aren't you dead? I left you for the dog to finish!"

"But Bruno's my friend," I said, which set her off again, until Mr. Rosenstael, wearing an expression of fastidious distaste, slapped her with great precision once each way and left a full imprint of his hand on both cheeks.

Cora gasped and whimpered and shut up.

"There's no money in the chest." I winced as I got to my feet, having banged both knee and elbow in falling. "Cora got it all. Nearly two hundred thousand. A thousand, two thousand a month. Because Margaret Foster couldn't keep her secret about how, so she thought, she had fooled the experts. She told her old friend Cora all about how silly men were, and Cora put the arm on Joe almost at once. Didn't you, Cora?"

Cora Whitney glared. Then, obscenely, she giggled. "Margaret wouldn't pay," she observed in a reminiscent tone. No, Margaret wouldn't. The repeated lie was her tool.

I remembered Belmont Street's surprise at Margaret's sudden death and the last piece of the puzzle fell into a gap I hadn't realized was there. "You killed her, didn't you, Cora? She wouldn't pay, but Joe would, and you killed her so she couldn't stop Joe.

A small, secret smile slid over her features. "It was easy. A few little pills in her tea. She always took it very sweet. I knew she wouldn't notice."

"But Joe paid, and once he started paying, he couldn't stop."

"All those checks to cash," mused John Wyndham.

"Exactly. He paid for upwards of nine years and the well was beginning to run dry, when he wrote it all down for his own safety. It's usually the other way around, but sometimes a blackmailer murders his victim to shut him up because people still go to jail for blackmail. So Joe wrote down the— all the details. Then he hid the paper. He must have told Cora, because after that it was a standoff. He couldn't stop paying and she couldn't raise her hand against him. After he died, Cora lost no time looking for that paper. What did he tell you, Cora? How much did he say?"

"He tricked me," Cora Whitney said in a voice of ladylike grievance. "He said—" She made a petulant gesture and fell silent. After a moment, "It's very difficult for a woman alone. She needs all the help she can get. You didn't suppose I made enough from my little shop to live on, did you, dear?" The faded brown eyes opened very wide. Cora Whitney might have been explaining deportment to the romper set. Another silence, while her gaze turned inward.

"He said—" she began again, and again broke off.

Her next sound was a scream. Hugging herself and rocking back and forth on her chair, Cora Whitney screwed her eyes shut and screamed, eldritch, maniacal screams that went on and on with inhuman regularity. She was still at it when the police took her away.

15

I SOLD THE Eastlake chest to Mrs. Montgomery for a hundred dollars. She's very happy with it, and I was glad to be rid of it.

Ray Foster doesn't come to Belmont Street anymore. I haven't seen him since the night Cora Whitney came unglued. There's a "For Sale" sign in one of the windows at Joe Foster's house. It will be interesting to see who buys it.

Pete, on the other hand, I see every day. Pete, strong enough to hold out for a grown-up love. No Lancelot, with an invisible horse in the background. Just Jiminy Cricket Pete, beloved.

"It's a good thing you never could see the horse, toots. You couldn't have told them apart."

Also, last week I saw the highboy, gaining admittance by a bold stroke. I phoned ahead and asked.

Abby Granger is a very old woman now, ninety at least, and she's in a wheelchair from arthritis. I suppose time hangs heavy. I could hear a dry, old voice in the background while I jousted with the officious accent that answered the phone. When Officious hung up, on a hunch I dialed again. After twenty-seven rings Officious couldn't stand it.

"—now about that appointment—"

"I told you Miss Granger could see no one. She must Have Her Rest."

In the background, "Good Lord alive, you make me sound dead. I'm not dead yet, I'll thank you to remember. Let me talk to her." The dry, old voice spoke in my ear. "What do you want, Miss Whatever-your-name?"

"Beckett. The name's Beckett. Susan Beckett, Miss Granger."

"All right, Susan Beckett, I understood you the first time."

I chuckled in spite of myself. The gutsy old girl! "Your trick, Miss Granger, pick up the cards."

"What do you want?" Her voice was several degrees less frosty.

"I want to see the Chippendale highboy you bought ten years ago from a Margaret Foster."

"I don't sell my furniture."

"I don't want to buy it. I only want to look at it."

"Why?"

"You bought the highboy, Miss Granger, on the strength of its having been authenticated by Dr. Henry Beckett—"

"What if I did? Good man, Beckett. Knew his job."

"He was all of that, Miss Granger. He was also my father. He's dead now, Miss Granger. The highboy was the last piece he ever vetted, and I'd just like to—to pay my respects. To Hank."

The old-fashioned phrase felt right. I wanted to see what Hank had seen, and seeing, at last say my good-bye.

The silence continued so long that I wondered whether she would hang up, but the line hummed open between us. I waited.

At length, in a voice surprisingly gentle, "Are you there, Miss Beckett?"

"Yes," sadly, "yes, I'm here."

"Silly question, wasn't it?" Miss Granger recovered her élan at a bound. "Tomorrow, about two-thirty, Miss Beckett. I'll make Mattie give us some sherry."

Very good sherry it was, too, as were the thin little unsweet cookies that appeared at the same time. After we ritually ate the cookies and drank our sherry, Miss Abby Granger shooed her companion into limbo and let me push her chair through wide double doors into the highboy's presence.

154

I caught my breath when I saw it and stretched an involuntary hand, before I remembered our bargain and snatched it back. Nothing had been said about touching.

"It's all right to pet it if you want, child. I often do."

I cast her a grateful glance and moved close to stroke the satiny figured mahogany, and then stepped back to view this magnificence from first one angle and then another. Everything about it was right, from the powerfully clutching claw feet and the artfully scrolled apron to the carving scattered like fine lace across the top and rising into the center finial in a frivolous ornament of the same lace shaped and stiffened by a cunning hand.

"Vetted very fine Philadelphia Chippendale highboy." I repeated the familiar words softly, and felt my eyes sting.

"What was that, Susan Beckett? Sounded like a quotation."

"It is." I tore my gaze away from the highboy's glories to meet old eyes, alive with unquenchable interest in life's goings-on. "It's what Hank wrote in his journal the day he appraised this highboy."

"Well, don't cry about it, child." Abby Granger was brisk. "He said it all, didn't he?"

I hadn't thought of it that way. Always, up to now, I had lamented Hank's parsimonious use of words in his last—no, next-to-last—journal entry. He might have said a *little* more than he did. My eyes went back to the highboy.

"Yes." I smiled at her, suddenly glad that Abby Granger owned the highboy. She and Hank would have understood each other. "He said it all." I gave her my hand. "Good-bye, Miss Granger. Thank you for letting me come."

Good-bye, Hank, I added silently, *it's okay now.*

"You're welcome, child. Please come again."

I saw that she meant it, and so promised that I would. Then I let myself out and hailed a cab back to Belmont Street.

155

If you have enjoyed this book and would like to receive details of other Walker mystery titles, please write to:
Mystery Editor
Walker and Company
720 Fifth Avenue
New York, NY 10019